Aethlon (*ăth-lŏn*): the original form of the Greek word meaning "prize of the contest; reward, recompense." We like to think of it as also including the notion of the contest or struggle itself (*aethlos*), and skill or excellence (*arete*) that wins the prize.

Aethlon

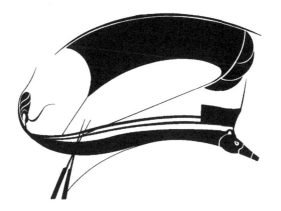

AETHLON: THE JOURNAL OF SPORT LITERATURE

Aethlon: The Journal of Sport Literature is published biannually by the Sport Literature Association. The journal is available to individuals and institutions through membership in the Sport Literature Association or by subscription from the Association. Single copies and back issues are also available from the Association. As a condition of membership, members in the Association receive a subscription to *Aethlon*, conference proceedings, discounts for the annual conference, occasional publishing discounts and membership in *Arete*, online discussion group. Membership rates for one year are: individuals $70, students and retirees $30, international individuals $80 and institutions $150. Single issues may be purchased for $25. Life memberships are available for $400. All subscriptions begin in Fall with issue number one. Memberships and subscriptions are for one academic year (August-July). Correspondence concerning membership and/or subscription should be addressed to: Joyce Duncan, Sport Literature Association, P.O. Box 70270, ETSU, Johnson City, TN 37614.

Inquiries concerning permission to quote or reprint from Aethlon should be directed to Joyce Duncan, Managing Editor [joyced1001@cs.com]. Books for review online should be sent to the Book Review Editor, Duncan Jamieson, Department of History, 401 College Avenue, Ashland University, Ashland, OH 44805 [damieson@ashland.edu]. Fiction manuscripts should be sent to Scott D. Peterson, Department of English, University of Missouri-St. Louis, 470 Lucas Hall, 1 University Boulevard, Saint Louis, MO 63121 [sdpeterson1890@gmail.com]. Poetry manuscripts should be submitted to the Poetry Editor, Ron Smith, 616 Maple Street, Richmond, VA 23226 [smithjron@aol.com]. Critical and Creative Nonfiction should go to Michele Schiavone, Marshall University, 1224 7th Street, Huntington, WV 25701 [schiavon@marshall.edu]. The author's name should appear on the title page only to facilitate refereeing. Manuscripts should be double-spaced, should avoid footnotes and endnotes, should follow the MLA Style Sheet (classics manuscripts excepted) and should be accompanied by a self-addressed, stamped envelope. Electronic submissions are preferred. Except for non-English quotations, manuscripts must be in English. Submission of .pdf illustrations is encouraged but not required. Authors are responsible for obtaining copyright permission for all items in their manuscripts. Articles published do not necessarily represent the opinions of, and are not the legal responsibility of *Aethlon*, The Sport Literature Association, or East Tennessee State University.

Printed by: Sport Literature Association with support from
East Tennessee State University, Johnson City, TN 37614-1000

Indexed by the Modern Language Association, The Humanities International Complete,
ThomsonGale, Ebsco, Proquest, and LA84

Aethlon: THE JOURNAL
OF SPORT LITERATURE

Contents

Opening Day

Scott Palmieri

It had to be about baseball. So many of his homilies were, and Mrs. Miller loved the game so much. But when Father McKenna looked at the pews, scattered with fewer Genevans than he had hoped, he questioned again the eulogy, which he had wrestled with ever since he heard the news of her death, but because of her beloved Geneva Knights, it had to be about baseball.

* * *

Mrs. Gail Miller eased her Buick LeSabre into her usual spot by the rectory, the brakes squeaking, as she budged the car into Park, hoping not to startle Father McKenna, the sturdy old priest, who was leaning a stepladder against the side of the adjoining church. Though no improvement projects in the works, the ladder stood as a reminder to the St. Francis parishioners that faith alone would not sustain them, with collection baskets already getting lighter, as summer approached in Geneva, New York.

Opening Day was finally upon her and the Knights, the city's summer college baseball team. Every year, Father McKenna gave the annual invocation, in the Knights' locker room, and for his efforts, the parish would take home half of the team's cut of the 50-50 raffle. He dropped into the passenger seat, content to give the rest of this June day to the Knights and Mrs. Miller, who was the head of all Geneva Stadium operations.

"Morning, Father," said Mrs. Miller.

"Morning, Gail," said Father McKenna, smiling through the dark sunglasses covering his squinting blue eyes. "Looks like we got a nice day."

"Sure did. Last year, we weren't as lucky," said Mrs. Miller, recalling the storm that blew in from Seneca Lake and rained out last year's home opener, when her annual picnic relocated to the cramped locker room—for the players, their best meal of the summer.

Meanwhile, Billy Gaffney was toweling off, after his shower, in the guest room of Mrs. Miller's house, in the Geneva Welcome Trailer Park she called home, pulling up his black mesh shorts over the padded whites of his sliding shorts. The night before, Mrs. Miller repeated her offer to the Knights' second baseman.

"You probably want to be with the guys, but you're more than welcome to stay, Billy," she said.

"Thanks a lot, Mrs. Miller. Yeah, maybe. I'll probably check out the dorms after the game," he said, the word "maybe" a polite gesture. He looked forward to having his own room at Hobart College, just a few miles from Geneva Stadium. A week before, he told a few of his new teammates of his temporary arrangements, as they dressed in the locker room before practice.

"It's a trailer park," said Gaffney.

"Really?" asked pitcher Joe Camgemi.

"Wheels or cinder blocks?" asked fellow hurler Ken Barton.

"What?" asked Gaffney.

"Can you drive it, or does it stay in one place?" asked Barton.

"No, it's like a house, no wheels," said Gaffney.

"Oh, then you'll be fine," said Barton, grinning back to his locker.

After the team's first practice, Gaffney returned to Mrs. Miller's house to find a small turd at the foot of his air mattress, courtesy of Champ, Mrs. Miller's old brown terrier, who yipped and limped about the trailer, relieving himself in unconventional places. Gaffney decided then that he was destined for the dorms, in a week's time, when they opened for the team. But hearing "maybe" gave Mrs. Miller hope, as she smiled at the short, slight middle infielder.

"Well, the room's all yours if you feel like staying. That's where the boys always stayed," she said. Gaffney noted her frequent references to "the boys," a reference to the days of host families, when there were enough volunteers to take in the players. In her first summer hosting, she awoke one night to the creak of the screen door, unabashed footsteps and banter, with Champ's piercing bark. In the weary light, she found her boarder, a smiling Mike Maconi, seated at her small kitchenette table, lifting a can of beer.

"Mrs. Miller, come join us!" he said, while a teammate next to him shuffled a deck of cards and another inspected the fridge for a post-midnight snack, their laughter revealing a long night at the Wagon Wheel, the local dive bar, on the outskirts of downtown Geneva. It was a thrill Mrs. Miller hadn't felt since she was a teenager, when her sister, Joan, would let her tag along, when Joan and Annie Doogan would smoke Pall Malls in her Chevy Impala, singing "Hound Dog" or "Louie, Louie" out the open windows, as they cruised Geneva Avenue.

Mrs. Miller took the can of Natural Light and sat. Maconi tried to teach her the game of "pitch," alongside these road trip vets, who had played countless times, across bus aisles, on flipped baseball buckets. Mrs. Miller couldn't quite get the hang of the bidding and incessant card tossing, though she let out a cheer when she and Maconi finally won a hand and the boys leapt to a standing ovation. The game lasted into morning, and Mrs. Miller awoke from a brief sleep, her elated exhaustion lifting her to slip through the small house and start breakfast. From that summer on, Mrs. Miller kept a milk bottle on her Formica kitchen counter, a painted baseball on one of the bottle's sides. The loud coin-to-glass clinks of early fall would give way to late spring patter, as the change packed closer to the top and another season returned, when Mrs. Miller would bring the heavy metal stash to the local Geneva Savings Bank. Her annual cashing out funded a dinner at Perkins diner for her host player and kept the fridge stocked with cold cuts. When another pitch game came, she would be ready.

One night, another summer, hopeful for another night of revelry, she awoke to a couple of voices. One teammate was cackling at the other, who was peeing on a fern in the corner of the family room. Champ barked until the stocky catcher zipped up. But Mrs. Miller never cast out a fellow sinner, especially one of her boys. She tossed out the fern but kept the catcher.

* * *

On their drive to the field, Mrs. Miller and Father McKenna discussed the most recent pastoral council meeting, where the priest was routinely challenged by the parish's most faithful, usually in handwritten letters, the most recent critiquing the Sunday Mass music: "The piano player is spotty, and the cantor's voice is flat."

"It's not like we can roll out the Beach Boys, you know?" said Father McKenna.

"Oh, don't listen to them. There's always some to complain about," said Mrs. Miller.

The two had met forty years before, when Father McKenna presided over Joan's funeral. On a July night, a truck driver fell asleep on I-90 and pushed Annie Doogan's car off the highway, killing Joan and Annie, when the car tumbled over. It was only Father McKenna's second funeral, and because Joan was so young, he struggled with what to say. During his meeting with the family, he learned of their love for baseball. The priest, too, was a big baseball fan, allowing him to follow Monsignor Wooden's advice about homilies: *find a metaphor.* Joan and Gail both played softball in the town rec league and attended minor league games at McDonough Park, later renamed Geneva Stadium, where the Red Legs played, in the days of Pete Rose and Tony Perez. It was the first of many metaphors he would try over the years, when he said that Joan was running home to Jesus.

They weren't all winners, though, telling the congregation how often we're caught in a pickle, or that studying the faith is like swinging two bats in the on-deck circle. He regretted most the Palm Sunday homily, when he likened Peter's denials to three strikes. Monsignor Wooden joked later, "Were they called strikes, Father, or did he go down swinging?"

As they pulled into the Geneva Stadium parking lot, they could smell the buttery breeze of cooking oil. Mrs. Miller scooted from the car to the concession stand, fumbling the keys to the lock. Matt Rizzo had forgotten to flip off the fryers the day before, when the staff reunited at the park to make sure everything was ready. She wouldn't tell Charles Dinkweather, though the team owner would have fired the teenaged Rizzo, for sure. For the moment, the only casualty was an emptied propane tank that she exchanged for another. Father McKenna leaned on the counter, as Mrs. Miller pulled the chain to roll up the metal shutter.

"Always some kind of disaster," said Mrs. Miller, shaking her head, with a wry grin.

"Thank God they have you, Gail," said the priest, as the warm salty breeze subsided.

"Always some disaster," repeated Mrs. Miller, smiling, shrugging her shoulders. As the stand aired out, she unlocked the box office to make sure the small shack behind the home plate grandstand was stocked with a wheel of red paper tickets and enough dollar bills to make change for the three-dollar admission. Next to the cash box, she pressed two pieces of silver duct tape on the laminated list of complimentary seats, which included Dinkweather, his family and some associates from Dink Soda. It also included Gary Stedman, sportswriter for the Finger Lake Times, who seemed to take pleasure in the team's perpetual struggles, most likely due to Dinkweather's attempt to have Stedman fired, after such headlines as "Knights Get Jousted," "Knightmare," and "The Holy Fail."

By this time, Gaffney had settled into his clubhouse locker, pulling up his uniform pants, whiter than they'd be all summer, a purple line hemmed from top to bottom, white patches sewn on the knees by Ginny Kershaw, from the local tailor shop, where Mrs. Miller picked up the uniforms after their annual mending. The players, still strangers, riffed like jazz musicians, around the common rhythm of pre-game banter, before Coach Davy's entrance.

"OK, guys, let's finish getting dressed," said Davy. "We have Father McKenna here to give our opening prayer."

"Ask him to bless your slider, Barton," said Camgemi.

"And he said, '*Take this cup and wear it,*'" said Barton, the lapsed Catholic holding the hard plastic shell like a Communion host. "'*This is the cup of my jock strap.*'" A couple of altar boy jokes were tossed like baseballs flung around the horn, until Father McKenna entered, the last of the players clipping their belts, then shuffling to the middle of the room to bow their heads beneath the priest's raised right hand.

"Dear Father in Heaven, look over these boys this summer, as they play this wonderful game, yet another gift that you have given us. Keep them safe and may they play with an open heart and giving spirit." When Father McKenna exited, Barton blessed the locker room: Gaffney's cleats, the bathroom sink, a tube of Ben Gay.

* * *

At Mrs. Miller's funeral, Barbara Cullen finished her reading from the Book of Lamentations, and the church pianist, Donny Devers, whose playing had not improved the past few years, stumbled into the opening notes of "Shepherd Me, O God." The cantor, Mary Ann Rice, while in her unsurprising flatness, beckoned the congregation with her impatient, aggressive gesture of participation.

Father McKenna noted again the sparse crowd and then the second row where Bruce Miller sat, arms crossed, impatient with the rites. "He's a good boy," Mrs. Miller would say of her "Brucey," as she called her son, any time the priest inquired. Bruce had dropped out of Finger Lakes Community College and after "having a tough time," as Mrs. Miller would explain, took a job as a cook at Scramblers, a small diner in Utica, where Mrs. Miller sent him money every month, though Bruce rarely visited or called. She had long given up on a grandchild. Before this week, the last time Father McKenna saw Bruce was at Ed Miller's funeral, following the lung cancer diagnosis and the four months that took Mrs. Miller's husband at fifty. When Ed's death was near, Father McKenna couldn't help but think of the imminent homily, an occupational hazard, like a tailor sizing up shoulders. Decades before, Ed was a star pitcher at Geneva High School, so baseball made sense again, but he struggled to find comforting words for Mrs. Miller.

Not until then did he think to use his favorite baseball cliché, what would become his 42 Regular: getting out seven of ten times makes you an All-Star. Even the best lives are full of suffering—Ed's agonizing end, Joan's death, Bruce's middling life, and even the miscarriages, which she shared with him, matter-of-factly on a walk, just days before Ed died. And regardless of his choice, right before Father McKenna began his homilies, he would gain strange courage by something else Monsignor Wooden once said: "It's amazing how much we get to say yet how little will be remembered."

* * *

After the locker room invocation, Father McKenna rejoined Mrs. Miller, beneath the tin roof of the picnic area behind the concession stand.

"Notice the field, Father?" she asked.

"Looks great," he said.

"The infield dirt is all brand new. No more lips. No bad hops here!"

"Wonderful."

"Rick Delaney rolled the entire field," she said, shrouding the tables with white plastic tablecloths, smoothing them out before taping the corners. "No lips here, either," she smiled.

For all of this, Dinkweather paid her 500 dollars for the summer. "Under the table," he would like to boast. Dinkweather, whose focus was on an elusive winning season, bristled at her one opening day request, though he agreed to pick up the helium-filled balloons Mrs. Miller had ordered from The Party Palace.

This attention to detail made her beloved at Sirens Travel Agency, where, for a decade, she worked as a secretary and the unofficial coordinator of all non-work activities. She tacked a birthday calendar on the bulletin board of the small lunchroom, the wall cluttered with curled photographs of May breakfasts, baby showers, and Christmas parties, along with a copy of The Sirens Daily Newsletter, which ran monthly, edited by Mrs. Miller, who detailed the branch's progress toward quota, along with notes about the new fax machine, the baby births, and reminders of Thirsty Thursdays at Clappers Bar and Grille, or the July picnic at Seneca Lake. All these activities ended when Mrs. Miller was let go, part of the downsizing that saw her and her fellow secretaries, "my ladies," as she called them, fired one by one. Since then, she took on temp jobs and volunteered at St. Francis running the spaghetti suppers. The few bucks from Dinkweather, along with Ed's modest pension, were enough to get by.

Dinkweather pulled into the parking lot, and as he stepped from his car, the pack of balloons escaped, blowing over the grandstand over home plate, where Jimmy Lockwood, about to finish his batting practice swings, saw Barton in dead center field, pointing hard at the sky. With a stiff breeze, the sack sailed toward left field.

"Stay fair! Stay fair!" yelled Barton. The players all stopped, as did Coach Davy, and turned toward the outfield. Lockwood laid down his bat and shuffled up the first baseline, peering to the distance, his hands like Carlton Fisk's in 1975, as if trying to push the balloons fair over the Green Monster.

"C'mon!" someone cheered.

"Get out!" yelled another.

"Way back, way back!" announced another in a play-by-play voice. "If it's fair, it's gone!"

Camgemi turned and straddled the left field foul line, watching like a third base umpire. The balloons, high above them, swept past the fence, holding inside the yellow foul pole. Camgemi pointed fair, and the players erupted, as Lockwood leapt, curling into a homerun trot around first base, giving a Kirk Gibson chainsaw-pull with his right fist, receiving howls from his teammates.

"Goddamnit!" yelled Dinkweather, slamming his car door, the balloons now a small cluster of dots in the vast bright blue. This is what Mrs. Miller had waited all year for.

"Always some disaster," Mrs. Miller muttered, stifling a laugh.

After batting practice, the players rounded up the balls spread about the infield. Gaffney caught sight of Mrs. Miller, leaning against the dugout, holding her clipboard and smiling at the boys. He wanted to steer clear the rest of the night to avoid another offer for him to stay, but he nodded and pursed a grin, as he descended into the dugout. He had known women like Mrs. Miller all his life, haunting his father's real estate office as a boy, twirling in the leather chairs to the adulation of the secretaries. They were his co-workers, during summers and semester breaks, when he answered phones and filed closing papers, bantering with his charm, aware of how much they would miss him, with his exit each fall for college.

Before the game, the public address announcer Tad Davis introduced the players, each one on the first base line, tipping his cap to the crowd, before Nicole Greenville, high school soloist from Geneva High School, nasaled her falsetto through the "Star Spangled Banner." When the game started, Mrs. Miller barely looked at it, shuttling from task to task, helping Robbie Winslow, the stadium's jack-of-all-trades, with the 50-50 and the between innings contests—the Dizzy Bat, The Flag Race, the Ned the Knight Chase—and directing the shaggers, children who dared the parking lot or the light traffic on Lyceum Street to retrieve foul balls for one-dollar coupons at the concession stand. With all that, she took joy in hearing the snap of ball hitting wood, the sudden jagged cheers and end of inning sighs, giving way to the warm-up songs, her favorite "Willie, Mickey and The Duke."

The Knights lost the game, a modest loss at that, 3-1, nothing too alarming. For Mrs. Miller, it was the post-game picnic that mattered most. The players emerged, still sooted from the game, the dirty uniforms piled into the laundry bin, which Robbie would bag and put in Mrs. Miller's trunk, to drop at Ginny Kershaw's. Each dish, quartered in aluminum trays and Tupperware, represented the Opening Day committee: Mrs. Cullen's garden salad, Mrs. Cameron's Swedish meatballs, Mrs. Drake's barbecued chicken, Mr. Jackson's homemade pizza, and Mrs. Miller's legendary red potato salad. Soon, the paper plates were cleared of food, save drips of ketchup, and it was time for Mrs. Miller to speak, her homily, as Father McKenna joked.

"I want to welcome you boys to Geneva," she said, as the players peeked up from their last bites, the sky above the picnic area and all of Geneva Stadium domed in the last of dusk's light.

"Every summer, you boys are out there, trying your darndest for us, and we want to make this summer a special one for you," she smiled. "You boys keep us young," she said, welling up, the crack in her words more severe with each summer. Besides Father McKenna, few players were listening to notice her gasp. Gaffney was, but an hour later, he was shoving his clothes in the cheap dresser drawers of his dorm room, his fleeting sense of guilt one of the endless benefits of youth, allowing him to ease back on his pillow and click on his Walkman, the *Eagles' Greatest Hits* gliding through the black felt of his headphones.

"So if you need anything, just give us a shout, and go Knights!" said Mrs. Miller, pumping her arthritic fist, as the players and members of the board gave polite applause.

After dropping off Father McKenna, Mrs. Miller returned home, the dirt driveway empty, as expected. When the storm door closed behind her, she heard the grumble of tires on the gravel road. Champ's bark marked their arrival. She saw a set of headlights turning into the park, switched on the lamp by the couch and pushed open the front door. Flashing a quick wave, her neighbor George Edison slid into his adjoining driveway.

The quiet of the trailer park bothered her, especially when her boys left. But there were nights toward the end of Ed's life, when she would thank God for it, when Ed's hacking fits would finally give way to a small cry and a couple hours of sleep. She thought she knew better to have hoped, even for a moment, that Gaffney would stay. But this was not a disaster. The picnic had gone well, she had Mass in the morning, and Monday was another game of many to come.

"I don't know, Father, but I feel this is gonna be a good season," said Mrs. Miller, earlier that day, before the first pitch, what she often felt with the baselines striped, the infielders smoothing the dirt with their cleats, and all the sounds returning, whose absence left her bereft the rest of the year. It would have been hard to imagine the ten straight losses to come or that a few months later, Dinkweather would sell the team to Line Drives, a corporate baseball company, who removed most of the staff and demoted the rest, Mrs. Miller's one last season spent in the box office.

After Mrs. Miller's death, a few years later, Father McKenna helped Brucey clear out the trailer. There on the counter was the milk bottle, the baseball almost all chipped off above a small pile of coins. The bottle gave him a fitting metaphor: the woman who gave so much, content with collecting the little she got back. Still, he wished he wasn't dwelling on her disappointments.

At the lectern, Father McKenna again noted the modest turnout—beyond a couple of her ladies from Sirens Travel and what remained of the spaghetti supper committee—but he grinned through his still sharp blue eyes. He had changed his mind again, now sure of what he wanted to say, aware of how few would remember.

"My brothers and sisters, today is Gail Miller's Opening Day."

The Pitcher

He nods to patrons even in upper decks,
and the cheap seats. Puffed in pinstripes,
two-toned bill shading his squint,
the pitcher crouches, winds up,
and fires a strike. Greased with pride's

precious liniments, thin muscles wrench.
At the center of it all, he sees from outside
himself: a golden-haired farm boy
who harnessed flash of speed, and power
to swat it out and trot the bases. After victories,

shoulders about the diamond, initials
crumpled programs for smart lads.
On the mound, bolstered with game-rage,
forgives his slow curve sagging just outside.
Searches down the pipe for an acceptable sign.

Batters dig in at home plate. He bleeds between
swings, unable to focus beyond the garland of grass.
Wind stirs, ravels old glories. Today, he relies
on deep center field's benevolence.
White-knuckle prayers. Knowledge grinds

in knees, his once-mighty right shoulder now stiff.
To survive the late innings he recalls the warrior myth:
under the lights, with the crowd who pardon
the next passed ball as he solicits another
grip and a perfect pitch in afternoon breeze.

Sam Barbee

Once a Runner:
More Than a Book about Running

David W. Atkinson

Perhaps the most widely read work of fiction devoted to distance running, John Parker's *Once a Runner* is the story of college athlete Quenton Cassidy and his ambition first to run a four-minute mile and then to defeat the world record holder. Originally self-published in 1978 and sold at track and field meets from the trunk of Parker's car, Once a Runner was for a long time out of print until picked up by Scribner's in 2009. Since then, it has continued to be enormously popular among runners everywhere, described as "the best novel ever about distance running" (Tracy, par. 1). Parker's book is, however, much more, and it is an oversight to limit the book in this way. Drawing on a variety of literary references and antecedents, Parker places Cassidy's experiences in the context of the quest narrative, and by so doing provides a rich appreciation not only of running but of life itself. Beginning with a brief discussion of why the running community is so enamored with *Once a Runner*, this paper discusses how Cassidy's story fits into the quest motif, how the book's characters enhance the quest story, and, finally, how Parker draws upon other literary works to provide additional depth to Cassidy's story.

There are several reasons for the novel's popularity with runners. Parker himself was a successful miler at the University of Florida, and there is no mistaking that running is a deeply personal experience for him. He understands the intensely competitive nature of the sport where "the swift blue runner is eaten by the slashing barracuda, which is eaten by the awesome mako shark" (Parker 15). He dwells on things interesting to runners: how many miles they run in training, who has run what times, who has bragging rights for the toughest workouts? Riveting is Parker's ability to describe the painful "distress" (223) of distance running, what he describes as the "deep ache that would all too soon become the ambulatory paralysis of the final straightaway" (261). There are, too, the many references to real runners. Jerome Drayton, Frank Shorter, and Ron Clarke, among others, are remembered and admired even today, thirty years after the writing of the book. While there is no such real-life runner as John Walton, anyone who knows the sport will recognize the New Zealand runner John Walker, who was the first person to break 3:50 for the mile.

Clearly, Parker keeps the running fraternity in mind in writing *Once a Runner* (Gibson, par. 10). But, fortunately, this is not all he does. Key here is how the novel is bookended by Cassidy's return to the track where he had his great victory against John Walton and where, it seems, he hopes to find closure on his running career. Cassidy begins his walk around the track in the opening pages of the book and concludes it in its closing pages. In between is Cassidy's story, framed as a quest narrative described as the "Trial of Miles" (11). In recounting the challenges Cassidy faces as a person and an athlete, *Once a Runner* shares much with the quest motif evidenced in everything from *Gawain and the Green Knight* to "Childe Harold to the Dark Tower Came" to *Lord of the Rings*. The story of the quest is associated with Joseph Campbell's *The Hero with a Thousand Faces* (1949),[1] and figures in any number of sports books from Malamud's *The Natural* (1952) to Abdou's *The Bone Cage* (2007).[2] Consistent with Campbell's idea of the monomyth, Cassidy leaves behind everything he knows in his quest to defeat John Walton and thus become the very best, what Parker describes as the "awesome mako shark" (15).

So, Cassidy, as the quest hero, aspires to the extraordinary. Early in the novel, Andrea, Cassidy's girlfriend, asks him, "is there some kind of final point to all this?" (63); his answer reveals that he is far from ordinary. Yes, he allows, we can "all be good boys and wear our letter sweaters around and get our little degrees and find some nice girl to settle, you know down with" (63). For Cassidy, though, ordinary does not exist; instead, he says,

> … we can blaze! Become legends in our own time, strike fear in the heart of mediocre talent everywhere. We can scald dogs, put records out of reach! Make the stands gasp as we blow into an unearthly kick from three hundred yards out! We can become God's own messengers delivering the dreaded scrolls! We can race dark Satan till he wheezes fiery cinders down the back straightaway …. We can sprint the turn on a spring breeze and feel the winter leave our feet! (63)

This is Cassidy's world; it is the domain of Arthur's Knights of the Round Table[3] and the quest for the Holy Grail, where few survive and even fewer find success. Defeating Walton is Cassidy's Holy Grail, and the implication is clear:

that many have tried, and no one has succeeded. Andrea says to Cassidy, "You are of course quite mad" (60), and there is indeed a madness in what Cassidy aspires to achieve. She recognizes that his "circuitry is all different" (194), that he is "a madman vexed and enchanted by ethereal considerations she did not understand…" (64). Cassidy's father asks, "what is it with this one?" (190), a rhetorical question for which there is no answer. In racing John Walton, Cassidy takes on a mythic figure, "an awesome creature—up until now more myth than mortal" who is to cross "oceans to perform his magic right on the same track that held their sweat" (57). In defeating Walton, Cassidy's victory becomes part of the same myth, something heralded by the "utter pandemonium in the stands as the chant degenerated into a howling, shrieking din" (266).

When Cassidy returns to the track at the beginning of the book, he thinks of September as "the month of promises" (2), a month when all things are possible. It is the beginning of his journey. As for all college students, September is the beginning of the college year and the hope for better grades and new experiences. For Cassidy and indeed for any college runner, it represents the beginning of the track season when new "best times" are to be achieved. In addition, it anticipates the "quest" story that follows in which Cassidy holds onto that promise as a way of getting through the challenges ahead. Finally, it is a comment on the outcome of the book when Cassidy realizes that there is "promise" for him after running.

As with the hero of any quest story, Cassidy's path is unrelenting, and he must be unwavering in pursuing his goal. "Slacking off" has no place in Cassidy's world. For Cassidy, there is no such thing as a missed workout; his diary tells "no lies and the symbolism of the unmissed workout became ritualistic to him, taking on an importance in his life he did not like to admit, even to himself" (35). Bruce Denton, who has traveled Cassidy's journey before him, is floored by the flu, but, even so, "he arose and ran two eerie miles at a stumbling pace, pale and shivering" (35) only to repeat the workout later in the day. The idea of "breaking down," the "cumulative physical morbidity" that makes "recover[ing] from one [workout] session to another difficult" (119) is seen as necessary to becoming faster and stronger. Cassidy, we learn, lives from workout to workout, hanging on like "a crazed marsupial on a branch in a flash flood" (125). Some might dismiss this obsessiveness as absurd and dangerous; as one commentator says, running 275 kilometers a week sets a "ludicrous precedent for those reading" the book (Fenton, par. 6). But Cassidy is more than a role model, and in his final race when he goes up against the world record holder, he experiences a transformative moment beyond what he ever thought possible.

Like other quest heroes, Cassidy must believe that the journey on which he embarks will be successful, even as there will be many doubts along the way. Cassidy must look into the abyss, a very Kierkegaardian thing to do, as he confronts the ultimate effort his running demands. And, of course, Cassidy's must be completed alone as he confronts not only the external demons of other competitors and the inexorable demands of training, but also the internal ones of doubt and denial. So it is that he retreats to Denton's cabin; only by himself will he discover who he really is as a runner and as a person. "On the trails," Cassidy ponders "what it mean[s], If anything, if anything at all (185). Parker makes a point of how Cassidy "began to feel like the lama on a mountaintop who is so finely tuned he senses the very food moving through his body" (178). Training is described as "a rite of purification" even as racing is a "rite of death" (122), not as physical death, but as the death of the old self for a new one. As in any quest, there is a moment when one confronts and vanquishes their demons. There might be an absurdity about the chapter entitled "The Interval Workout," in which Cassidy embarks on a workout of 60 quarter mile intervals. Runners and non-runners alike have commented on how no person could ever complete such a workout. But this is not the point. In his quest to be successful, Cassidy must be transformed, and he must do it himself. Significantly, Denton leaves Cassidy to complete the final twenty intervals by himself. Cassidy empties himself of all that limits him; on his last interval "he simply sprinted away the life in him. The thin silver of monorail that had once stretched out to forever now dropped off into a sheer abyss just over the horizon" (226).

The chapter ends with a puzzling but nonetheless tantalizing statement when Cassidy says, "it is a very hard thing to have to know" (226). What is "hard to know" is what Cassidy learns from the brutal workout—that beating Walton takes a very different kind of runner, one for whom there are no limits of any kind, physical or emotional. That no one recognizes Cassidy when he returns in disguise to race Walton (he has a beard and is outfitted as a Finnish runner from Central Ohio State), reconfirms that this is a "new" Cassidy. It is only when he challenges Walton on the track that the new "self" emerges, and the crowd recognizes who this mysterious challenger is. Cassidy knows he has the strength he needs; he talks about the "orb" that "floated gently in his mind," the still center that "would hold all grief, all despair, all race-woes of a body going to the edge." It would allow him "to do what he had to do until there was nothing left" (249). During his race with Walton, it is this "orb" that "bobbed gently, taking it in, retaining it, keeping it quiet inside the steely interior and allowing him to think" (261). As in any quest, the road is long to achieve one transcendent moment, when, as in Cassidy's race against Walton, he confronts "the decision for all time, the decision that would lead him up the path to higher callings" (262) as he moves "out to the second lane, the Lane of High Hopes, and ran out the rest of the life in him" (266).

Much of the criticism of *Once a Runner* focuses on how Parker writes about Cassidy's life away from track and field. There is merit to the complaint that some wanting only a novel about running will be frustrated by what they see as undeveloped and unnecessary characters and a disjointed narrative. Parker gives space to the shenanigans of the track team, and perhaps spends more time than necessary on the history of Doobey Hall, the designated residence for athletes. There is Cassidy's romantic attachment with Andrea, and the frustrations both feel about their relationship. There is the cruel joke played on Jack Nubbins, a self-important freshman runner, who is made to go through a contrived and cruel academic misconduct hearing in the Honor Court, orchestrated in large part by Cassidy. Finally, Cassidy is unwittingly drawn into an athlete's revolt against the Athletic Department and labeled a disruptive influence on team unity, the result being that he loses his place on the varsity track team and the opportunity of running against John Walton.

There are several obvious reasons for Parker's decision to write more than a running book. First, it would be almost impossible to write nearly 300 pages focusing exclusively on Cassidy's training and racing. Second, it is important to represent Cassidy as a student despite his commitment to running. There must be a life which Cassidy rejects in his single-minded endeavor to prepare for his race against Walton. Third, his dismissal from Southeastern's track team is necessary so that living and training at Denton's cabin becomes a possibility. Fourth and most important is that, while the novel has a sloppy narrative structure, it retains an organic unity in which the first half of the novel reveals much about Cassidy the person who figures so prominently in what Cassidy becomes as a runner.

It is true that the characters in Parker's book might seem insufficiently developed. But the simple fact is that in quest narratives, there is only one hero and everyone else plays supplementary, albeit significant, roles. The most important of these characters in *Once a Runner* is Bruce Denton, who serves in the role of prophet, a Gandalf-like character, who, having traveled the same path as Cassidy, provides the wisdom and support he needs. Denton's guidance is sacred; he is held "in secret awe" and "his words to comrades" are reported "with the solemnity of one reading from the Dead Sea Scrolls" (34). His workouts are "ritualistic" (35), and he possesses "secret" knowledge, a form of gnosis, which he imparts to Cassidy. It is entirely appropriate that Cassidy goes to Denton's cabin, a forest retreat which is different from anything Cassidy has previously known. Perhaps most important is that Denton has been to the top of the mountain; he is the "enlightened one" who knows how Cassidy feels and who can guide Cassidy on his journey, even as he knows that Cassidy must ultimately do things alone.

Others, too, figure in Cassidy's life. There is an immediate chemistry between Cassidy and Andrea and together they drift through the "pleasant cool eddies life . . . affords the young in fall and spring" (41). Theirs is a predictable romantic relationship, at once physical, highly charged, and fraught with youthful anxiety. In any quest, the hero must make a sacrifice. For Quenton, his feelings for Andrea are the one "true" thing in his life after running and it is this that he must give up. Their initial breakup is described as "meandering" and "half-hearted … a thing without reason" (194). But when Cassidy runs 12 miles from Denton's cabin in the rain because he is "missing" her (196), it constitutes a moment of conscious choice for him. Despite his obvious feelings, Cassidy denies temptation and does not pursue her when she turns away; instead, he runs the 12 miles back to Denton's cabin knowing full well what he is leaving behind. In other words, he knows that his goal demands absolute commitment. At the end of the novel, Andrea begins to understand, even if there remains a chasm between them. As Cassidy goes into the final lap of his mile race with John Walton, "something very deep inside her stirred as she realized that she was, after all, frightened for him, for this task he had taken upon himself" (265). It is this sense of task, one of incalculable enormity, that distinguishes Cassidy as a hero and an athlete.

Significant, too, is the graduate student Cassidy meets when Denton takes him to a faculty party. Eventually, of course, Cassidy craves human contact; he is still human, and he easily succumbs to her charms, a "cloistered monk turned loose among Manhattanites" (234). She remains unnamed in the chapter but still has a significant identity. She is the sorceress Morgana or Morgan La Faye, the half sister of Arthur, who exists in the shadows of Arthur's court and conspires to destroy it. Cassidy is reduced to nothing in her presence; he tells her "I have no moves left" (234). She is the one with "the dark, serpentine hand" and "carnivorous smile" (234) who seduces him. Parker's point here is not a complicated one. Cassidy's goal must be a single-minded one; there are too many temptations in the world that might turn him from his goal. Cassidy must return to Denton's cabin to complete his journey and prepare for his ultimate test against Walton.

Stephen C. Prigman, the President of Southeastern University, and Dick Dooby, the Athletic Director and Football Coach, are two characters who might seem out of place in a novel intended to be serious about running. While caricatures of what one might expect at a southern American college, they also serve as important foils for Cassidy. Prigman is ridiculed as a self-important good old boy, a former Florida Supreme Court judge noted for decisions which stand as "landmarks of jurisprudential comedy" (141). Dick Doobey, the Athletic Director and not very successful football coach, gets his job because of family connections and is presented as an overweight, not very bright philanderer who drinks too much. Both Prigman and Doobey define a deep-seated self-serving conservative mindset that allows for no deviation from the status quo. Prigman and Doobey are "rules" people who cannot allow for disagreement; they are driven by the need for security and predictability and want to hold onto a world that is theirs to do with what they wish. They worry about what others think of them and they do not take chances. By contrast, Cassidy is none of these things; he is prepared to give up everything to race against the world mile record holder. In this, he embarks on a quest that may ultimately fail. But because the prize is so great, he is willing to take the chance and to make the effort simply because not to do so would be to deny who he is. Simply put, Cassidy does not think as others do, and few can take on the task he does.

One final character deserving of comment is Brady Grapehouse, the athletic trainer for the Southeastern track team. He only gets one short chapter, yet he still serves as an important marker in the novel. We are told that Brady "is nearly a caricature of himself" (149). A trainer and someone who has been around for a long time and who has seen it all, he fits neatly into the archetype of the wise old man. He is the "ministering" angel who "with a look in his eyes … initiate[s] a deep understanding, forgiving and nonjudgmental, a look of someone who could not be shocked, who has his own agonies and wasn't ashamed" (150). As the single person trusted by the athletes, Brady allows for "no half-baked platitudes" (153) and demands that his athletes accept reality for what it is. Brady it is who "could, by God, get a man to talk straight to him" (151). It is significant that Cassidy when he is suspended from the team goes to Brady for support and advice, but never gets any because the training room is too busy. The implication is that the world of Brady Grapehouse is not where Cassidy will find his answers and is not where he will achieve his goals. Cassidy admits as much when he says, "There's nothing we can do about it now, so let's just leave it. I gotta get my run in" (154).

It is not a coincidence that Quenton Cassidy's name echoes that of Quentin Compson in Faulkner's 1929 novel *The Sound and the Fury*, an allusion described by one reader as an example of "the novel's goofy pretensions" (Tracy, par. 7). Be that as it may, it adds another level of meaning to the novel and is not to be dismissed. Both characters look for meaning in the world that explains the circumstances of their lives. Just as Quentin Compson bemoans the loss of his family and their southern status, Quenton Cassidy reflects on the loss of his status as captain of the track team. For Quentin Compson, time is an impediment; he remembers how his father said, "clocks slay time. He said time is dead as it is being clicked off by little wheels; only when the clock stops does time come to life" (Faulkner 85). He looks to stop time so much that suicide finally becomes his only option. Cassidy is also obsessed with time. In the chapter labeled "Time," he struggles with the slowness of time; he looks out from Denton's cabin "and wait[s] for time to pass" (192). More than this, he is consumed with the challenge of time, as he obsesses about his interval times in workouts and about what kind of lap times he needs to defeat Walton. The time on a stopwatch has the potential to be Cassidy's enemy, a reminder of his failure, of how he could not run the times he wanted. But it does not, as time ultimately signifies Cassidy's achievement.

Here one should note two passages in the novel, one at the beginning, and the other close to the end where time is front and center in the novel. Cassidy returns to the Southeastern track knowing that the "games were over for good" (2) referencing that the four years between Olympics is a very long time. But he also frames time in a particular way: "the passing of one minute took on all manner of rare meaning. A minute was one fourth of a four-minute mile, a coffee spoon of his days and ways" (2). The allusion is, of course, to T. S. Eliot's "The Love Song of J. Alfred Prufrock":

> For I have known them all already, known them all—
> Have known the evenings, mornings, afternoons,
> I have measured out my life with coffee spoons .... (ll. 49-51)

One might overlook this allusion (as many have) if it were not for the end of the novel. When Cassidy and Walton briefly meet after their race, we are told, "This is no game for upstarts or big surprises and Walton's look is clearly more of curiosity than anything else. There will be time, his eyes say, time for decisions and revisions" (269). Again, there is an echo of "Prufrock":

> There will be time to murder and create,
> And time for all the works and days of hands
> That lift and drop a question on your plate;
> Time for you and time for me,
> And time yet for a hundred indecisions,
> And for a hundred visions and revisions. (ll. 27-32)

Readers attracted to the book for its account of running might be forgiven for passing over these two short and rather oblique allusions. But they are important to an enhanced understanding of Cassidy as the runner everyone wants to be. Prufrock is an archetype for scrupulous timidity; he is getting older and is acutely aware of what he has become and what he has not achieved. He measures his life in coffee spoons"; he epitomizes the ordinary. Yet he still wants to "disturb the universe" (l. 46) and to make a difference; regrettably, he remains frozen; he sees himself as ridiculous and a fool.

> Politic, cautious, and meticulous;
> Full of high sentence, but a bit obtuse;
> At times, indeed, almost ridiculous—
> Alm ost, at times, the Fool. (ll. 116-119)

"Prufrock" provides a revealing context for Parker's novel. Cassidy returns at the beginning of the novel to the track where he ran his greatest race to be confronted with the hard reality that everything is finished. Like other Olympians, he looks back "tallying gains and losses" (2); he has little more to show than the endless quarter miles he ran in training. Like Prufrock, he wonders about what he has achieved, and where he is to go in the future. Cassidy, like so many athletes, fulfills his greatest dreams early in his life, and he is left asking the question, what now, does it get any better? Cassidy has only his memories, and the understanding that while one can remember the past, one "cannot experience it again" (3). One must "be satisfied with the shadows" and one must accept that "the shadows were sometimes quite enough" (3). Certainly, Cassidy has Prufrock-like qualities. Having experienced what few others do, he sees little in the future, frozen as he is in a life that allows for little else than running. After winning the race of his life, Cassidy thinks, *"I have nowhere to go"* (269), and on what should be a joyous moment of success, Denton reflects that "Quenton Cassidy's smile looked sad indeed" (269). Significantly, Denton has the same smile. Cassidy knows, as had Denton before him, that this single victory is as good as it gets, and everything else is anticlimactic. Prufrock asks the question, "And would it have been worth it, after all" (1. 87). This is also Cassidy's question. Have his efforts been worth it? We learn at the end of the novel that the ultimate prize eluded him. Having missed winning the gold medal in the Olympic 1,500 meters, Quenton is left with the realization that one does not win silver, one loses gold.

The reference at the end of the novel to "decisions and revisions" suggests a different outcome. It implies that Walton knows there will be other races and other opportunities, and indeed we are left with the feeling that Walton will exact his revenge. But it is also a reminder of future possibilities beyond running for Cassidy; he cannot succumb to the indecision that consumes Prufrock. Here the "huge Oak in front of Andrea's sorority house" (150) has particular significance. It has witnessed much over its three hundred years, and Cassidy asks himself, "What does this old fellow care about it all?"—that in the grand scheme of things, Cassidy's victories and disappointments do not shape a lifetime. It is telling that in the last sentence of the novel, it is this "very old, gnarled tree … Cassidy wants to find" and "then he would be on his way" (272). His colleges days are over, Andrea is gone, and his athletic glory is a thing of the past, but the tree remains as a reminder that the obsessions of youth cannot consume a lifetime. In the grand scheme of a lifetime, they are not worth it. As Cassidy warms up for his race with Walton, he is reminded of A. E Housman's elegiac poem "To An Athlete Dying Young," itself a powerful reminder that glory is fleeting; one cannot be an athlete forever and one's athletic achievements pass away to be surpassed by those who are faster and stronger. The message is clear: there comes a time when one must move on with one's life. Cassidy is not Prufrock's "fool." He gets to a place where the silver medal "no longer stab[s] at him" (272) and is no longer a reminder of his Olympic disappointment.

One might feel that Parker contradicts this ending by writing another book about Quenton Cassidy, who, enjoying a successful life as an attorney, feels he has unfinished business and embarks on an attempt to make the U.S. Olympic team in the marathon. One might hardly fault Parker for giving us more of Quenton Cassidy, as *Again to Carthage* (2010) is every bit as popular among runners as *Once a Runner*. As well, Parker chooses to give us an account of Cassidy before Once a *Runner in Racing the Rain* (2016), the story of how Cassidy discovers his running talents. But neither of these two books compromises how *Once a Runner* is more than a book about running. Perhaps it is not great literature, but Once a Runner possesses an organic wholeness that constitutes a compelling consideration of human drive and limitation and is an insightful consideration of the complexities of ambition. It is easy to see how Parker in writing such a readable book encourages readers, especially ones who are runners, to rush through it from cover to cover. But one must also realize that there is so much more to *Once a Runner,* and it deserves more than a hurried read. One in the end must be reminded of the title. Cassidy is "once a runner." Parker's book describes something of the past, that one can never be a runner forever, and that not to move on is to become Prufrock, frozen and unfulfilled.

Works Cited

Abdou, Angie. *The Bone Cage,* NeWest, 2007.

Carino, Peter. "History as Myth." NINE A Journal of Baseball History and Sport, vol. 14, no. 1, 2005, pp. 57-77. https://muse,jhu.edu/article/189388/pdf. Accessed Sept. 13, 2021.

Eliot, T. S. "The Love Song of J. Alfred Prufrock," *The Norton Anthology of English Literature*, edited by M. A. Abrams et al., 1962, W. W. Norton, 1968, Vol 2, pp. 1773-1776.

Faulkner, William. *The Sound and the Fury.* Vintage Books, 1984.

Gibson, Patrick. "*Once a Runner*: Unpacking the classic running book." Citius Mag., April 19, 2018. http://citiusmag.com/once-a-runner-examined/. Accessed Feb. 15, 2021.

Parker, John. *Again to Carthage.* Scribner, 2007.

_____. *Once a Runner.* Scribner, 1990.

_____. *Racing the Rain.* Scribner, 2015.

Phillips, Gyllian. "The Hero-Athlete Reconsidered in Angie Abdou's *The Bone Cage*," *Writing the Body in Motion*, edited by Angie Abdou and Jamie Dopp, Athabasca University Press, 2018, 107-122.

Tracy, Mark. "*Speed Reading: Once a Runner,* the best novel ever about distance running." *Slate,* Dec. 31, 2021. http://slate.com/culture/2008/12/john-l--parker-jr-s-once-a runner-the best novel you-ll-ever read-about-distance-running-html. Accessed Feb. 15, 2021.

Wasserman, Earl. R. "*The Natural*: Malamud's World Ceres." *The Centennial Review*, vol. 9, no. 4, 1965, pp. 438-460. https://www-https:// jstororg.ezproxy.macewan.ca/ stable/23737940?seq=1#metadata_info_tab_cccontents. Accessed Sept. 13, 2021.

End Notes

1. Campbell talks about the twelve steps of the hero although they can be generally summarized as the departure from home, the adventure, the initiation, an apotheosis, and a return to home.

2. Bernard Malamud's *The Natural* is the first and still one of the most prominent examples of sports fiction using the Arthurian quest as a narrative pattern. There has also been considerable discussion of how Malamud's protagonist Roy Hobbs gets his archetypal form from the youth of Sir Perceval. See "*The Natural:* Malamud's World Ceres," *The Centennial Review*, vol. 9, no. 4, 1965, p.40. For a more recent discussion, see Peter Carino, "History as Myth in Bernard Malamud's *The Natural*," NINE: *A Journal of Baseball History*, vol. 14, no. 1, 2005, pp. 67-77. For discussion of the "heroic monomyth" in *The Bone Cage*, see Gyllian Phillips, "The Hero-Athlete Reconsidered in Angie Abdou's *The Bone Cage*," in *Writing the Body in Motion*, edited by Angie Abdou and Jamie Dopp, Athabasca University Press, 2018, pp. 107-122

3. See, of course, Malory's *Le Morte D'Arthur*, in which Galahad was the only one of Arthur's knights to find the Holy Grail.

Photograph

I've never seen this one before.
The son of a deceased teammate
sent it to me, snapped
sixty-seven years ago.
A summer league team,
North Mississippi champions.

Shortstop and MVP in the playoffs,
I sit on the front row, Buddha-like,
as self-composed and confident
as when I hit the bases-loaded,
game-winning double in the final game.

The team is grouped
under a large tree that shades
the faces of Bob and Charles and Roger.
There was more shade to follow.
Expressionless beside me
sits the sure-handed first baseman
who would become my college roommate
and who would later know
divorce, bankruptcy, poor health,
an early death. Also on the front row
is the best player on the team, only one
good enough to play college ball, first
of the group to die. Half of those standing
on the back row, including our bespectacled,
professorial coach, are also gone.

We were all so young, so innocent,
but we walked through that summer
like princes. The whole town idolized us.
Who cared where the future led?
We were the unbeatables.

Robert Hamblin

Spiral

Salvatore Difalco

Vinnie had the big leg. He could punt the football almost fifty yards. Mind you, he was a big bastard, man-sized at thirteen, though he looked like a big galoot in these dungarees he had taken to wearing. He had played offensive tackle for our peewee football team, Stradwick's Lions, as well as handling the punting. I had played receiver but they switched me to safety after I dropped a few balls. But it didn't get me down as tackling suited me just fine. There was nothing like creaming a running back in the hole or hitting a receiver so hard he dropped the ball and spit out his mouth guard.

We stood in the middle of Eastwood Park hoofing the ball back and forth. Football season was a long way off, but first warm day of May we were out there hopping and high-stepping. It felt wonderful. It had been a long winter and sloppy spring thus far. The sky was high and blue despite the sulfur and soot spewing from the nearby steel mills. Vinnie's old man worked at Stelco. My old man had worked the coke ovens at Burlington Steel before he got sick. I couldn't help wondering if working there had led to the cancer. One thing I knew: I would never work in a steel mill, not in this lifetime, not if it was the last place to work on Earth.

A stiff breeze kept the usual rotten egg stench at bay. Some kid in blue-and-white stripes down by the abandoned brewery flew a red diamond kite with a white tail. Sprinting along the brewery's chain-link fence, he zigzagged the kite through the blue sky then stopped running and let it float there with little bobs and dips, the tail gently whiplashing. It took commitment to fly a kite. Pretty cool.

I could see my house from the park, its drab stucco brightened by the yellow tulips my mother had planted in the front yard a few days before. Her efforts to beautify the place depressed me. We were planning to move before my father got sick. My mother wanted to live in the west end, away from the factories and the lowlifes in our neighborhood. I didn't mind living here what with the park right across the street. No doubt you took your chances when you stepped outside your house and always ran the risk of catching a beating from some roaming gang or random thug, but it kept you on your toes. Never a dull moment, as they say. As far as I knew the west end was for pussies and posers. But among many things that had battered my mother's spirit during the last two years, the thought of being stuck in that house must have crushed her. She was no longer the bright-eyed happy woman I had known throughout my childhood, always singing and dancing and messing around. She'd become a shell of her former self, hollow-eyed and joyless. That I could do nothing to make her smile also pained me, for we had always shared a light and jokey relationship.

My nonna sat on the porch dressed in total black watching us with her hard black eyes. She had reached the point in her life where she approved of nothing, tolerated no one, and gave a fuck about very little. Living a hard life will do that.

"Kick it straight!" Vinnie yelled as he lumbered after a ball I shanked off the side of my foot. It rolled near a park bench. Vinnie grabbed the ball and sat down, huffing. He brought to mind a farmer having hauled bales of hay or something.

"Come on, fat ass. Kick it back."

"Go fuck yourself, Sammy. You kick like a little girl."

"And you're a big salami."

"Better a big salami than a little girl."

"And you might wanna change your clothes now and then, man. You've been wearing that garbage man's suit for weeks. The fuck is wrong with you?"

"Have you looked at yourself in the mirror lately? Your fucking nose looks like a hose. It's growing as I look at it. You're like Pinocchio."

"Go fuck yourself, Vinnie."

"Good comeback."

It was true. I had inherited my father's nose. Another reason to resent him. My only hope was that the rest of my face would grow into it, though that I saw that going terribly wrong. I took little comfort in my mother's adage that there is one nose for every face. I waved to Vinnie.

Taking his time, he stood up and ambled to a spot. He held the football out from his body with both hands and with a stiff right leg clobbered it high in the sky, so high I lost it in the sun. I held my breath trying to track it in the blaze. It seemed to take forever to come back down.

"That's how you punt a ball," Vinnie said, snorting and pumping his farmer arms.

"That was a beaut."

"Yes it was."

"Okay, okay."

"Now give it some leg, Sammy. Try to hit a spiral. It'll go higher."

"Yeah yeah."

Just then I saw Rosina the neighbor hurrying toward my house, her hooked face tight and her arms crossed on her chest. A bit of a busybody, if you asked me, showing up uninvited any hour of the day, thirsty for bad news or gossip, her beaked face bobbing, she reminded me of a vulture. Maybe I'm being harsh. She often brought over donuts she purchased at the little bakery near the soybean factory where she worked, usually a couple of dozen—granted they were day-olds—so how bad could she have been? My nonna no longer sat on the porch.

Something was going on with my father, obviously. Something was always going on with the fucking guy since he got sick with cancer two years ago. He had it in the lungs but it had spread to his spine and his brain, so he was pretty messed up and drugged to the max. In and out of the hospital a dozen times, each time seemed like it would be the last. But he was a tough nut; I'll give him that. Those old Sicilians are hard to break. He always came home from the hospital; a little worse for wear each time, but he wasn't about to die there.

My mother had purchased a black Naugahyde recliner on layaway from Sears so he would be comfortable after they removed one of his lungs and he couldn't lie down flat without almost choking to death. He could barely speak and spent most of his time upright on that thing, watching television, taking his meals, spitting blood or peeing into bottles. He'd get up to bathe or go number two with my mother's assistance, though a few times my sister or I had to help him, a task I hated with a passion. He smelled. I didn't like the smell of him. A little like pee and sweat and ass but also like something rotting, rotten.

My sister Angela, two years younger than me, had far more patience with him than I did. My father had always treated her more gently than he had treated me, though she had not been entirely immune to the occasional cuff or cutting insult. On which occasions her sorrow had the power to provoke immediate regret. But let me be frank, being sick didn't make the man any nicer or softer. You'd think he'd back off a little, adjust his temperament just a bit given his circumstances. On the contrary, just the week before, he had cuffed me in the chin for talking back to my mother about some small thing. Took me by complete surprise. Guy could barely lift his arm but he had the courage to cuff me. I didn't say anything, for the sake of my mother, who had fled the room in tears. I just took it, like I always took his cuffs and slaps and punches and fucking put-downs. And get this—the man wasn't even an alcoholic. He didn't even drink wine with his meals like most Sicilians. He didn't even have that excuse going for him. He was just mean—a mean fucker. Maybe life had made him that way, but more often than not you choose to be how you are, no matter what your past.

What can I say? I couldn't totally hate him for being the way he was. We are all products of our predispositions and our upbringing. I'd say he was predisposed to anger and pettiness—traits I detected in myself. But he was *old school*. And I reckoned that's how all those old school fathers were, some variation of my own father. And it wasn't really their fault. Their fathers had brutalized them from the sounds of it. Indeed, objectively speaking, they had softened their approach considerably from what they had experienced and learned. Still, even understanding this, explaining it away, perhaps even condoning it to some degree—as my long-suffering mother likely did—made it no easier to swallow.

He weighed about a hundred pounds now and I could have probably kicked his ass had I the hatred in my heart and wherewithal. But how bad would that have looked? Thuggish Teen Beats The Shit Out Of Dying Father. Good headline. And my mother would have never forgiven me, let's be honest, and that terrified me more than anything the old man could have ever done to me.

Uncle Joe pulled up in his red pickup truck seconds later. He sat there for a moment before killing the engine, then hopped out smoking a cigarette. He turned his head left and right, took a last haul of the cigarette, and tossed it among the tulips before mounting the porch steps.

He was a good guy, Uncle Joe, my mother's big brother, a good man. For my tenth birthday he took me to Buffalo for a Bills exhibition game against the Steelers. I was a big Steelers fan so I was stoked. The Steelers won, and after the game we drove to Niagara Falls, New York, and ate pizza and wings at Honey's. It was easily one of the best days of my life and I loved my uncle for it. Needless to say, my old man hated football. He hated all sports. If not for Uncle Joe—who paid the sign-up fee—he wouldn't have let me play peewee football.

"How much are they paying you to break your skull?" he would say, slapping his thigh. "What are you, some kind of chooch?" Stuff like that. I guess he didn't play any sports back in Sicily, after the war. Things were brutal there. They were too busy trying to find something to eat, too busy trying to survive. At least that's what he'd tell me. It made me feel a little sorry for him, but all that shit had nothing to do with me and didn't lessen my desire to play football. This wasn't Sicily, and we weren't exactly starving or scrounging for food.

I hoofed the football as hard as I could. This time I caught it in the sweet spot. It soared into the sky, spiraling to its apex, then plummeted down to Vinnie, standing there squinting with happy feet, arms cradled for the catch. The football thumped into his breadbasket. He secured it and gave a thumbs-up.

Wearing a lacy black kerchief in her black hair, Aunt Celestina now mounted the porch steps of my house. She slowly opened the screen door and stood there a long moment before entering. For a second I thought she was going to cross herself. She was the holiest person I knew. She went to church every day, every frickin day, and always had the rosary going. Her arrival added gravity to the situation, but I tried to block that from my thoughts.

"What's going on?" Vinnie yelled.

"I don't know," I said.

"Didn't your father just get out of the hospital?"

"Yesterday. Now kick the ball!"

Vinnie hesitated before he kicked it.

"Is he okay? Like, was he okay?"

"Just kick the frickin ball."

Was he okay? Was he okay? He was not okay and would never be okay. Was I going to say that? Maybe I should have. But maybe it would have made it real. Maybe it would have punched me in the mouth. This time the ball went off the side of Vinnie's foot and wobbled toward the rickety grandstands at the baseball field. Dust and debris swirled over the semi-abandoned diamond. I jogged over to get the football, cursing under my breath.

A dog barked across the street. I looked and saw Yogi Beager in a stupid bucket hat walking Rexie, his vicious German shepherd. I liked dogs, but not Rexie. Yogi was the neighborhood asshole and the dog had learned from him. Everything he did was to piss people off or fuck them up in some way, sour their day. For a second I thought he was going to cross the street and walk Rexie over. He knew how uneasy the dog made me feel. But he continued walking with Rexie and passed my house, pausing for a moment with a quick turn of his head before moving on.

A hand screening his eyes, Vinnie stood there looking toward my house.

"Sammy," he said. "You better go see."

I pretended not to hear him. He stared at me with his mouth open, judging me. But he didn't understand, I'd had it up to here. It couldn't always be about that shit. Guy was like a black hole, sucking the light and the life out of everything around him. I was sick of it. Every day it was something else. Every day. I couldn't breathe anymore. I just wanted to breathe. What the fuck was so hard to understand about that? I walked to the spot, squared up and hoofed the ball to him. It went straight up in the air. It went up so straight I could have almost caught it myself, but it thudded into a spot on the grass between us and bounced toward Vinnie.

"Sammy, something's going on."

My ears burned. "Like what? Like what do you think is going on?" I realized I was shouting.

Vinnie blinked. He was fighting back tears. "I don't know, Sammy. I think you should go see what's happening, though."

"I'm not going anywhere," I said. "Kick the ball."

Vinnie stood there with the ball in his hands. His face looked blubbery and pale in the sunlight. As I waited for the football, I glanced toward my house but only picked up the yellow blur of tulips. They made me sad. I found them unbearable. I found it all unbearable. I looked toward the brewery to see what the red kite was doing. It must have crashed down—the kid walked along the fence with it crumpled and twisted in his hands, his head bowed. Life sucks, kid.

When the ambulance pulled up without a siren, Vinnie said he had to go home, that I should, too.

"I'm not going anywhere," I said.

"I'm taking the football."

"Don't do it."

"Sammy."

"I said don't take it."

"You just gonna kick it by yourself?"

"That's right."

He tossed me the football and loped off.

I moved to the back of the park, near the brewery fence, where the kid had been flying the red kite. No sign of him now. He was off somewhere hating the unfairness and cruelty of the world. I squared up and kicked the football. It flew left. I could hear my name being called. I retrieved the football and squared up again. This time it went straight off my foot. You have to kind of catch it sweetly on your instep.

Eventually they stopped calling my name.

Slaughterama

Because Ed's armband tattoo was fresh and bled
its geometric repeating waves beneath the clear bandage
of Saran Wrap on his bicep, only I'd compete
in the annual bike event called Slaughterama
that year. Each spring, in Richmond, Virginia, hundreds
of crust-punks, sculptors, musicians, bike messengers,
baristas, grad students, tattoo artists, and other
heavily pierced locals toting six-packs of Pabst
descend on Belle Isle to watch the games. To get
to the island from the city's north bank, you have to cross
a suspension footbridge slung by steel cables
that sway over the muddy James. The games
are part carnival, part demolition derby
held in the tin-roofed ruin of Old Dominion
Iron and Nail Works—an open-air factory-shed
that resembles a rectangular horse arena. That spring's
competitions: tall-bike jousts, bike-chariot races,
conceptual tricycles, and unicycle boxing
with raw chicken tied to participants' hands
like gloves. And there's always some

shirtless bartender named Marty with a pentagram
squirted in Heinz 57 on his beer belly: one way
he helps his friends find him in the crowd. Ed,
my first college boyfriend, was a pot dealer
and glassblower of blobs so lumped and solid
he sold most of his art objects as "paperweights." He'd
introduced me to Slaughterama on one of our first dates.
Ed of the eye-twitch and white-boy dreadlocks that reached
his lowest vertebrae. Earlier that May, he'd helped me weld
two bike frames together to make a double-decker ride
so I could compete in the tall-bike jousting event
in which mounted participants lunge toward each other

grasping the extended ends of toilet plungers
like medieval lances. Since Belle Isle once housed
thousands of starved and lice-bitten Union soldiers
in the island's Civil War prison camp—whose grit
and silica now swirl through bicycle spokes—some
Slaughteramans wear thrift-store navy blazers in homage
to the dead's blue uniforms as a way to give
the finger to the Confederacy. The unofficial mantra
of the games: *Cheating is encouraged,* which means
people try to shove you off your bike or pelt your arms
and back with empty Pabst Blue Ribbon cans. *Even losers win—*

the games' other mantra, which I learned
firsthand when I didn't last a full minute
jousting a wiry woman with a half-shaved black bob
who shoved her toilet plunger hard into my right boob
and I toppled from my giant bike to the dirt.
People raced over, cheered, and poured their beers
on my forehead's crown and into my open
mouth, grabbed my wrists to raise my arms
into a victory "V." Ed pulled me up, his saran-
wrapped tattoo leaking a waterier ooze
as he kept drinking. I shook from adrenaline,
my left shin stripped of skin along four inches
of bone. But getting bloody with hundreds
of others was part of the fun

and also part of the dark edge that crept in at dusk
as the games ended. I could tell time by the state
of Marty's ketchup pentagram, which smeared and shed
its dried lines, changed shape over his stomach
like a sundial's moving shadow. The wounded bikers
would limp in a hooting troop back over the footbridge,
leaving Belle Isle's paths spattered, the leaves
of sweet gum and sassafras smudged as they
must've been some nights in that other century.
Sometimes a lucky biker would leave with the misshapen

lead mushroom of an antique bullet she'd picked
up and tucked in her pocket. I always hoped
to find one. That night I bandaged my shin while Ed
replaced the crusted saran wrap over his tattoo
with new layers, slept with that same arm
draped over my nude waist. His wound oozed for hours,
leaked a beer-thinned streak into my belly button.
When I woke I found in my innie a dried
red plug the shape of a thumb.

Anna Journey

Fighting Female:
The Portrayal of Femininity in
Fighting with My Family

Morgan Riedl

The World Wrestling Entertainment (WWE) is a media company best known for its production of professional wrestling but has extended its reach into other venues, including a film studio, WWE Films, founded in 2002. Its embrace of the genre "sports entertainment" combined with a move to market toward a broader audience places the WWE's wrestling in the same category of analysis as TV programming, more generally. Indeed, seemingly in line with the WWE's goal of becoming more mainstream, in 2019 WWE Films released *Fighting with My Family*, a drama-comedy inspired by the real-life story of WWE wrestler Paige. This film itself is based on the 2012 documentary, *The Wrestlers: Fighting with My Family*.

This foray into traditional media overlays an additional layer of representation atop that of the athletic performance and, underneath even that, the cultural performance of gender, as philosopher and gender theorist Judith Butler posited. Wrestling's hallmark is its performativity and storytelling. And then the film is a story about a story; the WWE is essentially telling a story about itself and (re)defining its brand in the process. This is to say, there is Saraya-Jade Bevis, the real-life woman who plays the WWE character of Paige; then there is Paige represented in the WWE events; and then there is the film (inspired by the documentary) which represents both Saraya-Jade and her character Paige. So, the film is in some ways constrained by Saraya-Jade's real life and by the existing characterization of Paige, which is mediated by the WWE, in how it represents both characters. Still, within these limitations, the filmmakers can and, indeed, do refine gender representation to appeal to their widening audience. Thus, an understanding of gender gleaned from the film will inherently be refracted, a few times over. Nevertheless, a close reading and critical analysis of how the film negotiates gender representation reveals existing gender norms and how much the culture is willing to see them bent, particularly in the world of wrestling.

Being a Woman

This paper does not have the space for a comprehensive analysis of the creation of gender and gender norms, but philosophy and gender studies professor Sandra Lee Bartky's application of Foucault's principles of discipline to femininity is relevant here. As she explains, herself drawing from Iris Marion Young, women are expected to be "far more restricted than men in their manner of movement and in their spatiality" (Bartky 66). One of the ways this is manifested is in containing women's bodies by keeping them thin and weak (64-65). Wrestling certainly disciplines bodies, and women's bodies differently than men's, but it also creates opportunities for transgression of some of the aforementioned norms, as I will show. Women are not just allowed but actually encouraged to be freer, even wilder, in their movements; to take up space and both vocally and physically demand the right to inhabit that space; and ultimately to be powerful and showcase their strength.

A Matryoshka Performance: From Sports to Entertainment and Beyond

Wrestling has always existed in a contested space. Early in its history, the "realness" of wrestling was often in question, as promoters attempted to hide that the matches were scripted. However, women's and gender studies professor Betty Jo Barrett and social work scholar Dana S. Levin explain that in the 1980s the World Wrestling Federation (WWF), seeking to extricate itself from athletic commissions' oversight, publicly acknowledged for the first time that wrestling's "outcomes were predetermined" and thus it was not a sport but "sports entertainment" ("You Can't" 470). This newly-created category aligned wrestling with other physically demanding performances, such as theater or dance or acrobatics wherein performers use their bodies to tell stories. This blurring between "real life" and entertainment is further complicated, as freelance writer and sports journalism lecturer Carrie Dunn discusses, by the fact that the WWE uses "real-life events in storylines" that make the fiction hard to separate from the reality (2). While this essay is not interested in parsing out an answer to how much of professional wrestling is real or in defining reality, it is interested in how professional wrestling's representation of femininity impacts the world off the stage.

Existing scholarship examines the storytelling of the WWE, investigating the portrayal of both romance and violence. Indeed, much has been said about the violence of wrestling and its impact on cultural attitudes toward violence, especially violence as a trait of masculinity and violence toward women, some of which will be relevant to this analysis, but only so much as it informs wrestling's representation of gender. Additionally, violence in the WWE has been moderated in the last decade to such an extent that wrestling cannot compare to the top sources of violence in the media. Barrett and Levin trace in great detail the WWE's evolution over time, noting that in 2008, the WWE transitioned into a "PG era" during which it was "re-package[d] as family friendly entertainment" ("What's Love" 561). Because of this shift in audience, the violence and overt sexism were scaled back. Still, as will be examined, less obvious forms of misogyny continue, and, it should be noted, the least noticeable forms of sexism can be the most dangerous since they exist unrecognized, thought of as natural inevitabilities in the culture.

Making a Man(,) not a Woman

The substantial research on wrestling's messages about masculinity highlights the disparity of research on its messages about femininity—other than the important implication that a dichotomy exists. Overall, the scholarship shows that wrestling's definition of manhood supports hegemonic masculinity. In her research, sociology professor Danielle Soulliere identifies six messages about what wrestling says it means to be a man, including "(1) real men are aggressive and violent, (2) men settle things physically, (3) a man confronts his adversaries and problems, (4) real men take responsibility for their actions, (5) men are not whiners, and (6) men are winners" (8). While not all of these are inherently problematic, some of them certainly are—the encouragement of violence and emphasis on a type of success that depends on another's failure—and all of them contribute to the dominant definition of masculinity, which anxiously guards inflexible categorical boundaries with room for only a single kind of masculinity to be considered acceptable and capable of signifying a "real" man. Additionally, in the same way that success is defined in the binary of win/lose, these traits are defined in contrast to femininity, so that "masculinity is constructed in opposition to femininity" (6). In these cases, femininity is defined by what it is not, and, moreover, its traits are being assigned an unfavorable status. For example, if men are not whiners, then women are, and being a whiner is not valued. Thus, femininity is given an innately inferior status.

Building on the first message about masculinity being that men are violent and aggressive, Barrett and Levin studied inter-gender violence in WWE narratives and find "three core themes": "(a) females as perpetrators of retaliatory physical violence against males, (b) males as perpetrators of physical, verbal, and sexual aggression to intimidate females, and (c) justification for female violence against men behaving badly" ("You Can't" 475). Their analysis of what violence is permitted based on the gender of the perpetrator and victim shows that "benevolent sexism" has replaced overt sexism, and that it "reinforces patriarchal gender relations by constructing women as dependent on men for safety" (484-485). Women might no longer be victims of violence but often remain the targets of intimidation. When a woman is threatened, another man might step in to protect her or she might act herself. But women's aggression is permitted as a response only. A woman who is aggressive "by nature" would be pathologized in a way a man would not be. Unprovoked aggression from either a man or woman might be reprehensible, but wrestling reveals that the culture accepts the former as natural. Moreover, men are expected to be the provocateurs, to confront and, thus, escalate a situation. While wrestling articulates parameters for acceptable violence, the expectations are gendered, with stricter constraints on women's behavior even in the fictive world of wrestling where their violence is showcased.

Wrestling with Women

Although most scholarship on the WWE focuses on men and masculinity, some recent analysis has focused on women, or Divas, in the WWE. As Dunn finds, women usually occupy supporting roles, which might contribute to the lack of attention paid them; regardless, she claims it is a result of the WWE being "uncomfortable with 'women fighting'" (13). Indeed, women fighting would challenge cultural norms about femininity, and given the WWE's shift to the mainstream marketplace, this would present an obstacle to drawing in a wider audience. So, instead, in order to be Divas, the WWE expects women to be "sexy, smart and powerful," and Dunn compares the combination of these specific traits to female bodybuilders who balance physical strength with more "'traditional', 'typical' heterosexually-aligned displays of femininity" (14). Similar to defining femininity in opposition to masculinity and creating inherent subordination, this expectation that women be "sexy" positions gender in line with other dominant cultural narratives, notably heterosexuality. This is to say, men decide what classifies a woman as sexy, and to be sexy is to appeal to men.

Romance in wrestling narratives has been decidedly heterosexual. Barrett and Levin identify six core themes in romance narratives in wrestling, which reveal "conflicting and complex ideas about the nature of heterosexual romance" ("What's Love" 565). The lack of any same-sex romance is notable for it reveals the heteronormative framework of wrestling storylines. The absence might explain why little work has focused on queerness in wrestling or attempted queer readings of wrestling narratives. The absence also might be understood in light of film historian and LGBT activist Vito Russo, who examines the conflation of non-normative gender presentation and non-normative sexuality in media (16-19). Indeed, it is possible that anxiety around perceived queerness compels wrestling to reinforce its strict gender norms, on the assumption that masculine men and feminine women will not be read as queer. Thus, Divas must present as normatively female and be seen as heterosexual, a view underscored by the heterosexual romance narratives.

Even in the face of reinforcing patriarchal gender relations and heteronormative gender roles, a more optimistic view of the rise of the women's division is possible. Sociology scholar Rachel Wood and media and popular culture scholar Benjamin Litherland employ a "critical feminist framework of hope" in a close reading of the documentary *WWE 24: Women's Evolution* to examine how the franchise's reference to popular feminisms and celebration of neoliberal feminism serves as a positive opportunity, especially given the sexist history of the program (910-916). The film openly criticizes that problematic past, which highlights how the promotion has evolved and how it is continuing to evolve in line with feminist principles. Indeed, women's place in wrestling has improved in line with how women's place in the wider culture has improved; though, in both spheres, disciplining forces still seek to constrain femininity and limit how far a female body can step outside gender norms.

Fighting in Films

Much media research has focused on martial arts more so than wrestling. Film studies scholar Yvonne Tasker examined Chinese martial arts films and their westernization for messages about race, masculinity, and sexuality. She finds fights in Chinese martial arts films to be both sensuous and aggressive, that they put the male body in a "feminine position" not because the characters are feminized but because they become objects of the gaze in the same way that women are often subject to the male gaze, as theorized by British film critic Laura Mulvey. Tasker goes on to say that these films "stage homoerotic fantasies, primarily working through … white male sexuality" (506-7). While her analysis is examining race which this analysis is not, her observations elucidate the position the wrestlers occupy in relation to the audience. All performing bodies are objects of the gaze, and in wrestling that gaze is male, not just because the audience is predominantly male but because the performance is created (imagined, scripted, cast, practiced, directed, etc.) in the context of a culture that privileges, often unknowingly, this particular gaze. Women are expected to be fantasy objects for the male gaze, hence the directive they be "sexy." Men, meanwhile, are also made objects of this gaze, and so to preserve (presumed) heterosexuality, the male wrestlers must anxiously assert their masculinity in opposition.

Additionally, women's and gender studies professor Lisa Funnell traces the representation of women warriors through time, looking particularly at the appropriation of Asian culture and themes. One of the early tropes she identifies is that of the "television warriors" of the '90s who are feminine but capable and whose storylines are ironic and playful (Funnell 97). Play and comedy are central to the WWE film and tools which serve to highlight gender norms. While both Tasker and Funnell focus on race and neither speaks specifically about wrestling, their studies' examinations of gender in TV and film help contextualize the representation of femininity in the WWE film in question, showing how historically media has portrayed women who fight. I will examine how the film both continues to follow traditional scripts for femininity but also negotiates new boundaries for women.

Femininity in Fighting

The WWE film *Fighting with My Family* follows siblings Saraya—Raya, for short—and her older brother Zak as they grow up performing in their parents' wrestling company, called a "promotion," in Norwich, England, and attempt to make it into the big leagues by joining the WWE in America. In the movie's opening scene, child-Zak is watching WWE on TV and Raya changes the channel to Charmed (more on this choice later), which causes the siblings to fight. Zak puts her in a wrestling hold, and upon hearing the kids' shouts, their parents walk in. In the first instance of ironic humor, the parents react unexpectedly, encouraging their children's play-fighting by asking Raya what she is going to do—she responds with a series of maneuvers that gets her out of her brother's hold and puts him in one. The film's use of comedy often operates by playing on gender expectations, which calls attention to what is otherwise invisible. For example, the parents encouraging the children to wrestle garners laughs because the audience expects the parents to stop the fight and perhaps punish the brother. But, more importantly, the scene elicits laughs also because the parents explicitly encourage their daughter to respond by wrestling, which the audience does not expect. The culture assigns physical aggression to masculinity, so parents are expected to prune not promote that trait in female children.

The audience's introduction to Raya establishes, at least in part, how the movie will treat her femininity specifically and femininity more generally. Earlier it was noted that Raya attempted to watch the TV show *Charmed*, a supernatural series about three sisters who were good witches. It gained a cult following while it aired on the WB from 1998-2006 and, even after its end, has continued to be referenced in pop culture. The show is recognized and understood by the audience to be gendered feminine. By making Raya a fan of the show, a fact that the film references later, she is characterized as feminine also. Given later moments when her gender is explicitly questioned or mocked, her love for *Charmed* serves as an anchor for the audience to understand her "authentic" self. The audience does not have to wonder if Raya is a "real" girl when those moments arise. By showing that even as a child Raya is interested in what society expects girls to be interested in, the movie normalizes her gender and essentializes it. It depends on the audience's belief in the permanence of gender—so that whatever gender Raya is as a child will be the same gender Raya is as an adult. These choices to normalize, essentialize, and permanentize Raya's gender likely go unseen by a mainstream audience and result in the creation of a character this audience finds understandable and acceptable.

The scene continues as the parents push their wrestling promotion on Raya who seems reluctant, but her mother steps in and affirms Raya's beauty on both the outside and inside. The scene then cuts to Raya wrestling her brother in front of a crowd that is enthusiastically cheering her on. After she wins, she throws her head back and arms behind her and screams wildly. At this point, the scene cuts again to the future, jumping ahead several years, when Raya is in the ring with her mother in another wrestling match. In these scenes the film continues to carefully negotiate Raya's femininity in line with audience expectations. At first, she is shown as concerned with beauty and not wanting to wrestle. It is the feeling of victory and positive reinforcement from the crowd placing her at the center of attention that seems to change her mind. Nevertheless, her gesture of victory, the abandonment with which she reacts, the loudness of her scream, all push the boundaries of traditional femininity. As explained above, Bartky finds, at least outside the ring, that girls are expected to be contained, passive, and quiet. Raya ignores all that—taking up physical space and being vocal—and is able to get away with this mild transgression on the wrestling stage. In this way, wrestling creates space for expression that is slightly non-normative. The film seems aware of how setting influences behavior, by portraying Raya as loud and aggressive within the boundary of the wrestling arena, deeming it acceptable there, but perhaps not elsewhere.

The first time Raya's gender comes under scrutiny is while she is passing out flyers advertising her family's upcoming wrestling match. She approaches three passersby who present as very typically feminine: blond, thin, wearing dresses, etc. After Raya invites them to the match, they decline. When pressed, one mentions that wrestling is for boys, then wonders aloud if she has misgendered Raya for that reason, asking, "Are you not a girl?" They ask if she is in costume and refer to her family as "weird." The exchange comes to an end when, after more insults, Raya finally threatens to shove their heads up their butts. From there, the scene cuts to Raya examining herself in her bedroom mirror. Because Raya's gender has been established for the audience already, they are not put in a position of questioning it. Additionally, by showing Raya examining her own gender expression, the audience is made to understand that Raya wants to be seen as a girl and that the earlier exchange has made her question the success of her performance of femininity. Even though her clothes aren't particularly "girly," she isn't attempting to transgress gender but rather just be herself, and that self is female.

Raya's presentation is worth considering in detail here. She dresses almost exclusively in black, which matches her long, straight, usually loose, black hair. She wears heavy, black eyeliner and has a lip ring. Her wrestling outfit, consisting of black booty shorts, sometimes fishnet stockings, and combat boots, reveals a fair amount of pale skin. Her style might be called "punk" or "emo." This reinforces a reading of Raya wanting to be herself, still a girl but her own kind of girl, pushing back against what is popular among girls but not pushing far enough to enter androgyny. Indeed, in the insult noted above, her family is labeled "weird," not "queer." This idea of being one's "true" self is furthered a few scenes later when Raya and her brother Zak encounter Dwayne "The Rock" Johnson at their local tryouts for the WWE. Dwayne Johnson is a famous former WWE wrestler turned actor, who stars as himself in (and produces) the film, further complicating the layers of representation mentioned earlier, and in the fashion of the WWE, blurring the boundary between storytelling fictions and the facts of life. Raya and Zak ask him for advice on how to become the next Rock. He responds by telling them instead, "Be the first you." The film supports the popular encouragement of "be yourself," though the extent of protagonists' non-normativity is minimal. This is to say, the message seemingly is to be yourself as long as you aren't too different. To your own kind of woman, as long as your femininity is recognizable.

During an interim training scene, a boy gets an erection while working with Raya. The moment is played off as humorous, as the dialogue reveals that this boy commonly gets "stiffies" while wrestling with her. The boy's attraction to Raya is notable because, in a heteronormative society, femininity is partially defined by what attracts men. As explained earlier, Dunn finds that WWE Divas are expected to be "sexy." This scene is consistent with Dunn's analysis as this boy being turned on by Raya shows she is sexually desirable to boys, thereby affirming her femininity. Still, Raya's sex appeal isn't exploited, nor does she exploit it, as might be expected given the recent trends in the characterization of warrior women that Funnell discusses. That said, Raya's characterization seems in line with Funnell's "television warriors" of the '90s because she presents as fairly feminine but also as physically capable. Her gender expression is not hyperfeminine, though, and assumes some masculine traits.

At the tryouts, the wrestlers are asked to introduce who they are and explain why they want to join the WWE. During Zak's explanation he catches himself using a curse word and says, "Oh, I shouldn't swear when there are ladies present." The audience believes he is referring to his sister, the only girl at the tryouts, but Zak turns to the male wrestler standing on his other side, who has very long hair. It is another instance of the film's ironic humor playing with gender. Though it's not clear, it doesn't appear Zak misgendered the man intentionally—still, the audience experiences the misgendering as funny for a few reasons that reveal their gender expectations. First, the audience thought he meant his sister, and the fact that he did not shows he doesn't think of his sister as a girl. Second, his misgendering of the man as female is humorous not just because it is wrong but because it is demeaning. Whether Zak meant it as an insult or not, the audience understands that calling a man a woman is offensive, and—whether or not the audience is aware of the reason—this is because the female gender is considered the second sex. Summarized earlier, Soulliere found in wrestling that masculinity was defined in opposition to femininity, with feminine traits being seen as undesirable. In this way, Zak not seeing his sister as female is meant to indicate he sees her as an equal. While on an individual level this might be beneficial for Raya, on a systemic level it reinforces the gender binary and patriarchal devaluation of the female.

During Raya's introduction at tryouts, she must pick a new wrestling name. She has used "Britani" but, as the WWE representative explains, they already have a Britney. Raya chooses "Paige," her favorite character from the TV show *Charmed*, a reminder of her femininity. The audience can recognize that her different names represent her different selves on a literal level: Raya is her real-world self and "Paige" is her wrestling self. Beyond that, Raya's multiple identities afford her opportunities to transgress expectations. In the ring, for example, "Paige" can behave violently, whereas Raya is limited in the "real world" by law and gender norms. For example, as Barret and Levin explain, a woman who is thought to be aggressive by nature would be pathologized ("You Can't" 478). Raya can be aggressive only when it is for a purpose—when she is "Paige" participating in a wrestling match. Still, the multiple identities are not fully separate and at times collapse into a singularity. In the same way that parts of the identity of "Paige" are drawn from real-life Raya, Raya might find that acting as "Paige" informs her own real-life identity. During her explanation for why she wants to wrestle, she says her whole family wrestles and it's what she's been doing since she was thirteen. When the representative asks again, she sassily repeats her answer. When he asks a third time, she answers that it's an escape from the real world. Raya gets to escape society's constraints and be "Paige," which may be a truer self since the identity offers her more freedom to be who she wants.

Ultimately, Raya is selected to go to the next level of competition to get into the WWE, while her brother is not. This reveal is not unexpected—given the plot and characterization, it is almost predictable. However, this is still a reversal of sorts, as more typically the boy would be expected to excel at wrestling. The film plays the role reversal up even more by juxtaposing a later scene in which Raya is bench-pressing with a scene of Zak's girlfriend giving birth to their child. Raya is becoming the superstar athlete while her brother is becoming a parent, challenging the expected gender roles of man as athlete and woman as mother.

During the WWE training, women are featured as the focus of shots, positioned more prominently than men. While Dunn's research shows that women have traditionally played only minor or supporting roles in the WWE, this film places women front and center. Perhaps this is only because the film is about a woman's rise in the promotion and thus must focus on the Diva division to the exclusion of the (male) Superstar division. Still, when Raya arrives at Florida for the next round of competition, she meets the three other main women who are portrayed as competitors even though there is nothing to suggest that only one person will ultimately get the contract. The presentation of these three women recalls the scene of the three girls who mocked Raya when she passed out flyers. By normative cultural standards, they are beautiful, showing off their tanned, thin, and toned bodies in bikinis by the hotel pool. Compared with them, Raya is not as sexy; though her sex appeal has already been established, relatively, she falls short. They are introduced as the stereotypical cheerleader, model, and dancer (their previous professions)—beautiful but not smart, in direct contrast to Raya. At this point in the narrative, the film seems to complicate Dunn's conclusion that Divas should be both sexy and smart as the three women are the former and Raya is the latter, but neither is both. Of course, none of the women has earned her place as a Diva yet, so each has a chance to develop the particular trait she is lacking.

During their interactions, it is clear the other women don't have wrestling experience. One accidentally hits Raya three times during a practice session. Raya finally slaps her, which she calls a "receipt," to teach the woman to pay closer attention. The WWE representative screams at Raya to apologize for the slap, which she eventually does. In a culture where women usually apologize for taking up space, Raya's resistance is notable for the confidence it reveals. Afterward Raya finds the three women during off hours, not to apologize sincerely as the audience might expect, but to "explain" the receipt. She accidentally ends up implying that the women are there to use their bodies to get famous, which causes her to be further excluded from their group. Her being ostracized can be understood to represent Raya's place on the fringe of mainstream culture and on the edge of gender norms as well. The culture encourages women to use the sexual appeal of their bodies, and Raya sees this as not true wrestling.

During a practice wrestling match in front of a crowd, Raya's liminal position makes her a target for her competitors as well as the audience. While the other wrestlers engage in trash talk, Raya can't find her voice to respond and, sensing her vulnerability, the crowd joins in, calling her a freak, Ozzie Osborne, and other names mocking her appearance. One even yells, "At least he's not in a bikini," explicitly and intentionally misgendering her to emphasize her nonconformity to conventional beauty standards. After the show, Raya cries and then takes action to conform to expected femininity by removing her dark makeup, taking out her lip ring, and dying her hair blond. The WWE representative asks her if someone broke up with her—again reinforcing the earlier mentioned heteronormativity, implying femininity is a performance for, about, or in response to men. As mentioned earlier, Russo examines the perceived connection between non-normative gender expression and non-normative sexuality, which suggests a similar connection between normative gender expression and normative sexuality. In this way, Raya's embrace of normative gender expression is interpreted as reflecting a normative sexuality or being a sign of sexuality in general. Raya's transformation calls attention to the performativity of gender while also reinforcing expected roles because even her earlier self, the one she changed, wasn't overly masculine.

Ultimately, the transformation doesn't help her in the way she'd hoped. On break from training, she flies back home to England not intending to return to tryouts. While at home, though, during a family wrestling match and subsequent conversations with both her brother Zak and her parents, she is reminded that wrestling professionally is her dream. She reverts to her original look, rejoins tryouts, and repairs her relationship with the other three women. Raya's embrace of her true style is a metaphor for an embrace of her true self. Her confidence that she can have her own version of femininity is strengthened. By teaming up with the other women, Raya also calls attention to and subverts the stereotype that women are catty and in competition with one another for men. The women express femininity differently but respect each representation. This is shown to make them better wrestlers because they can perform more advanced wrestling moves that require working in pairs. It is when the four women come together that they all seem sexy and smart and powerful—the qualities Dunn says Divas are expected to embody. This is also in line with what Wood and Litherland found in the WWE's recent inclusion of popular feminisms. Indeed, the film emphasizes female collaboration from this moment until the end.

The ending of the film begins when the trainees are taken to a WWE match. At the free-food buffet, Raya takes three hot dogs. Raya is able to ignore another instance of societal pressure to conform to the expectation that women meticulously watch what and limit how much they eat in order to stay thin, as Bartky explains. Before she can eat, though, she is whisked away so that The Rock can tell her she is signed with the WWE and will compete that night for the Diva title. Feeling the pressure, Raya calls her brother, saying, "I have no idea who I'm supposed to be." She explicitly expresses uncertainty about her identity, part of which is her femininity. Her brother tells her that it's okay to be the weird freak from England. He then comforts her by reminding her of a time when he was wrestling in his dad's shorts which were too big and fell down, exposing his penis to the laughter of the crowd. Nothing could be as bad as that, he insists. When he asks if she has her own shorts, she says, "Yes, my penis won't fall out." Part of the humor of her retort is that she doesn't deny having a penis. The gender bending of the language is safe, though, because it isn't true. Still, it does suggest the idea of so-called "Big Dick Energy" (BDE), which is self-assuredness that propels one to success. The phrase became popular in

2018 and comes from the idea that men with large penises are imbued with confidence so that they don't have to compensate with false bravado or by taking assertive action. While a fuller analysis of the term is beyond the scope of this paper, BDE isn't the prerogative of men; women can have it too. By claiming a penis, even if metaphorical, Raya is owning BDE. She is claiming the power and status of the masculine sphere while retaining her femininity.

The final scene is Raya's match with the title-holding Diva AJ. Raya looks the same as always—dressed in black—and AJ is dressed in a red pleather bikini, more typically feminine. The fight begins with AJ trash talking and Raya not responding, recalling the earlier scene where she choked in the face of insults. AJ then slaps her and starts pulling her hair. Upon being called a freak, Raya finally responds by taking her down to the mat and punching her. Their two fighting styles, at least at the start, seem gendered. Slapping and hair pulling are often associated with catfights, for example, whereas pinning someone to the ground and punching is the purview of men. That being said, Barrett and Levin focus on women's violence in response to men in matches ("You Can't 475-79). Since this fight is between two women, the scene complicates the authors' findings. There is not a male instigator or a male misdeed to justify their violence. Rather, their aggression toward each other is justified because it is in service to their goal of winning the title. Here, women can be independent, and female ambition is lauded, which further supports Wood and Litherland's hopeful reading of the WWE's progress while pushing back against Dunn's argument that the WWE hasn't fully embraced women fighting. Notably, the fight between the women does not have an explicit sexual subtext, as might be expected given Tasker's findings that such scenes are often crafted as fantasy for the male gaze. While the WWE itself may do this more extensively, this film does not play up sexuality as AJ and Raya fight, but it does allow the women to be sensuous and aggressive. Though their outfits are certainly revealing, camera shots do not emphasize their bodies but their wrestling instead.

Ultimately, Raya persists and emerges victorious, the youngest WWE Diva's Champion in history. She addresses the crowd, "I am a freak from Norwich, England, and I've dreamt of this my whole life ... this belongs to anyone who feels like they are the freak from Norwich ... those who feel like they don't belong!" The final screen cap reads: "Her popularity and influence helped usher in the 'Women's Revolution', gaining more respect and airtime for women of WWE." The film seeks to embrace a slightly different femininity than what is conventional. It follows the narrative tradition of elevating the "outsider," and locates some outsider status in femininity that borrows from masculinity. While femininity alone would be considered the lesser if situated against masculinity, any expression that does not fit into this binary is considered even less.

The film's representation of femininity reflects progress in the WWE's representation of women but also consciously improves upon it in line with popular feminisms. The movie's narrative is that of a woman's rise in professional wrestling, so by its nature it seeks to be empowering. Because the woman is a real person who starred in the WWE, her characterization must be at least minimally consistent with her WWE character, given the existing fanbase. And it strives to represent the real woman accurately, based on the documentary's representation of her. In its representation of femininity, the movie lauds feminine ambition and strength, traits usually gendered masculine. It showcases (scripted) female aggression and violence in matches, as well as female collaboration, further pushing back against stereotypes and normative gender expression. Despite its intentions, its portrayal of femininity does not greatly challenge the normative definition, even though the film commendably shows women can successfully wrestle and still be women and does make space for marginally non-normative femininity. This is not to discount the importance of these marginal shifts. Indeed, while this paper has chosen to focus on this one successful big-screen film, future analysis might consider the Netflix series *GLOW*, a dramedy about a female wrestling circuit, which aired for three seasons from 2017-2019, winning much critical acclaim and recognition, but which was canceled in 2020 after the pandemic complicated production. In the last few years, not only have women in wrestling deservedly received increased attention, but also the subject of women in wrestling has attracted more interest, affirming the importance of continuing critical conversations about gender norms and femininity in this arena.

Works Cited

Barrett, Betty Jo and Dana S. Levin. "What's Love Got to Do With It?: A Qualitative Grounded Theory Content Analysis of Romance Narratives in the PG Era of World Wrestling Entertainment (WWE) Programming." *Sexuality & Culture*, vol. 18, 2014, pp. 560-591.

Barrett, Betty Jo and Dana S. Levin. "'You Can't Touch Me, You Can't Touch Me': Inter-gender Violence and Aggression in the PG Era of World Wrestling Entertainment (WWE) Programming." *Feminism & Psychology*, vol. 25, no. 4, 2015, pp. 469-488.

Bartky, Sandra Lee. "Foucault, Femininity, and the Modernization of Patriarchal Power." *In Feminism and Foucault: Reflections on Resistance*, edited by Irene Diamond and Lee Quinby, Northeastern University Press, 1988, pp. 61 – 86.

Butler, Judith. "Performative Acts and Gender Constitution: An Essay in Phenomenology and Feminist Theory." In *Performing Feminisms: Feminist Critical Theory and Theater*, edited by Sue-Ellen Case. The Johns Hopkins University Press, 1990, pp. 270-82.

Dunn, Carrie. "'Sexy, Smart and Powerful': Examining Gender and Reality in the WWE Divas' Division." *Networking Knowledge*, vol. 8, no. 3, 2015, pp. 1-18.

Funnell, Lisa. "The Influence of Hong Kong in Hollywood: The Asianization of American Warrior Women." *In Warrior Women: Gender, Race, and the Transnational Chinese Action Star.* State University of New York Press, 2014, pp. 94-110.

Johnson, Dwayne (Producer), & Merchant, Stephen (Director). *Fighting with My Family* [Motion picture]. United States: MGM Studios, Inc., 2019.

Russo, Vito. "Who's a Sissy? Homosexuality According to Tinseltown." *In The Celluloid Closet: Homosexuality in the Movies.* Harper & Row, 1987, pp. 3-60.

Soulliere, Danielle M. "Wrestling with Masculinity: Messages about Manhood in the WWE." *Sex Roles*, vol. 55, 2006, pp. 1-11.

Tasker, Yvonne. "Fists of Fury: Discourses of Race and Masculinity in the Martial Arts Cinema." In The *Gender and Media Reader*, edited by Mary Celeste Kearney. Routledge, 2012, pp. 503-16.

Wood, Rachel and Benjamin Litherland. "Critical Feminist Hope: The Encounter of Neoliberalism and Popular Feminism in WWE 24: Women's Evolution." *Feminist Media Studies*, vol. 18, no. 5, 2018, pp. 905-922.

Heavy Bag

I'm moving around it
Slugging it toe to toe.

My right sinks in—
My left sings out.

I sing out blow by blow—
I slug and sweat and sing.

The chain rattles
To an uppercut,

A right hook,
A violent left cross.

And the leather glistens—
A mute canvas glistening—

And I picture a face
Of someone I hate.

And the chain rattles.
And the chain rattles.

And I slug and sweat and sing.
And I sing out blow by blow.

And I go to the shower
Light in my calves

Flicking jabs at the universe.

David Evans, Jr.

Lakota Rules

RF Brown

FIRST QUARTER: Condors 0 — Marmots 0

Tip ball, Wétu hears her uncles, mad-louder than even the thundering crowd. Lakota Nation's in the gym, crazy for basketball. Crazy for girls' varsity. Nation loves Wétu, their shooting guard. Her girl, Zuya, their power forward. This year, their senior girls might finally win everything. Tip goes up at Lakota Nation High, to the rafters filled with mad-excitement and down to the hands of their team. *For rez peeps,* Wétu thinks, *Friday night games is all they got.*

Lakota Nation High is mostly trailers. Gym's the nicest building for a hundred miles. Outside it's the poorest place in the USA. Lonely houses with no electric or plumbing or addresses. Flat dead dirt, mile after mile. Hot wind, nasty with chicken shit. Dry land sold to wasicu ag by the tribe desperate for pennies. Second hand shops, salvage yards. A thousand bars and liquor stores, and the restaurant is Fuel & Jug. The casino built for wasicu tourists, now full of natives, and all around it a border of road litter fouling Nation's kinship with the Earth. No trees. But, tonight South Dakota Girls Quarterfinals has come to the rez.

Wétu Brings Water don't look skinny like Lakota's cheerleaders. *Them three fat bitches only friends with each other. They got nothing either to be snobs about.* And she don't look long and complex like Zuya and her mile-long rope braid. Cheerleaders said Wétu's little braids make her look like a tribe boy. But her uncles say she got mad-speed on court. Coach Proudhorse, over half-glasses, says she got acrobatics. Zuya says Wétu got intense mahogany eyes. *What's mahogany?* Wétu keeps one mahogany eye on the three women refs. *One ref looks native, but she ain't from here either.*

Aberdeen Lady Condors never played Lakota's Lady Marmots—probably never played a rez-ball team. Lakota got fast run-and-gun. Blonde Aberdeen got expensive baby-blue uniforms, perfect white lines on their shorts. Wétu really don't like the one in the headband and sport goggles. *How do I say her jersey, MacDonahough? How do wasicu keep their socks so wasicu?* Marmot home whites look dingy compared. Wétu loves her girls, hates "Lady" Marmots. Nobody calls the boys Gentleman Marmots. *And them boys call us lez-ball. Don't give a fuck. Ladies? Alright—they boys.*

Her four uncles in the stands all have long old-school ponytails. All wear the same satin jackets from some tournament only they remember. They're ancient, but never miss a high school game. Holler embarrassing war whoops and fire invisible arrows at the Aberdeen visitors section every time Lakota fills the bucket.

Her unci's in the stands too. When the crowd jumps Unci sits in her wrinkled skin and wrinkled t-shirt sipping a plastic cup of beer. Unci don't like Zuya. She says, "Zuya runs like a man." "Zuya wants to turn you her way." *Some of the old ways are still good, some are just old.* Wétu loves Zuya, she's a star. Unci's one to talk bad influence, spends long days at the casino on no money.

First quarter Lakota attacks Aberdeen with hustle. Pass after pass. Keep them not knowing where the ball's going. *Just keep shooting threes even if our shots are bricks.* Crash the board with rebounders—four, five! Then full-court press on D., force turnovers. *Be aggressive, ladies.* Ball gets loose. Wétu dives for a floor scramble with the blonde horse MacDonahough. Shovey and spitty and double fouls. Coach Proudhorse, in her homemade skirt, fights her bench of Marmots from getting up to kick Condor asses. *Noise of Lakota Nation gets loose.*

Lakota up more than double at the eight-minute buzzer. *Eight million invisible arrows from eight generations of Great Sioux warriors rain down on the visitor's section.*

SECOND QUARTER: Condors 14 — Marmots 30

Ms. Proudhorse—third coach in four seasons. All her experience is on her clipboard. She's Lakota High's history teacher. Others tried to hold the girls with systems. Coach Proudhorse says, "Just play girls," and they're in the quarterfinals. Wétu just plays the rez-ball her uncles taught her since she was five.

Wétu knows fast breaks, not set plays. Get the ball, make a way to shoot. Run to the line—score three points from the top. Pass to Zuya in the wing— three pointer. Pass to Mima, pass to Kimi, pass to Wétu, to Zuya—cuts a layup. Every Marmot with the ball's a shooting threat.

Condors score a lot too. That's rez-ball. Surrender baskets, win on high score. Coach Proudhorse substitutes full squads. Quick breaths on the bench. Condors coach can't track who's on who. That's why she's yelling about cheaters. "They're palming, ref!" "You're not calling illegal subs!" "That's a Marmot elbow, not a Marmot kiss."

Sorry, lady, that's Rez-ball offense. Get out of the way or we move you. Get the money to the bank quick as possible. Make them chase. Defenders get there, dish off to Zuya in the wing, score off the glass. Ring your girls on the three-point line and fire. Miss? Rebound and fire back another three.

When they shoot, always assume they miss. When their shot's in air all five Lakota girls become mad-rebounders. Get the ball, transition fast, automatic points.

High school rules give a thirty second clock. Lakota don't need it. Possessions last ten seconds, six. Running back and forth on the court tires Condors. Refs get worn out too. Different basketball than Condors of Aberdeen ever played, but the rules are exactly the same. At the buzzer—Lakota up by twenty.

HALFTIME

In the hall where the team jogs across to the home locker room, they pass a glass case rarely noticed. The case is filled with the ornaments of Lakota Nation High history and Teton Sioux heritage. There is a cow-horn rattle and a cancega drum. A hand-painted rawhide box, called a parfleche, is an artifact of the tribe's nomadic era. There are few athletic ribbons or trophies, but one girls-basketball trophy, won by the team Wétu's mother played on twenty years ago.

Wétu's mother was an all-state starter too, awarded a basketball scholarship to an east-coast university. But the system and the new life did not work. Like every star rez athlete Wétu ever heard of, her mother dropped out and came home to the rez. For now, her mom is with a boyfriend in Idaho working at the casino of a different tribe.

Lakota Nation High has talented athletes every year, but their teams rarely go deep into state tournaments. Once the game leaves the rez, the rules seem to change.

In the locker room Coach Proudhorse looks above her half-glasses into the eyes of each player. "I see a team that can go all the way to state." "It's yours, if it means more to you than it does to them." What Coach Proudhorse does not know about basketball, she makes up for in encouragement. "Wétu Brings Water, keep getting to where you need to get!" "Zuya Young, keep working hard for shots!" "Everyone, always be ready to get in the game!"

On the chalk board Coach Proudhorse, the history teacher, writes the words *Pre-Columbian Ball Games*. The ten minutes of halftime are ticking. "Three thousand years ago ancient Maya civilization played a game called Pok-a-tok. In Mayan rules, there were two teams on a stone court and an eight-pound rubber ball. The men had to pass the ball only with their hips to score it through a vertical ring. Sounds sort of like basketball, right girls? Well, at the end of Pok-a-tok the losing team's captain would behead the winning team's captain."

Some of the girls laugh, but Wétu and Zuya shut them up. "The goal wasn't to defeat the other team, it was to earn the honor of being sacrificed to their Gods." Wétu raises her hand and tells the coach we don't get it. "Ask yourselves," Coach Proudhorse says, "what you're playing for. For tribe? A college scholarship? To be the star of your high school? Next week's semifinals are up in Sioux Falls, off the rez. Whatever's your honor, keep playing like tonight's the biggest night of your life. Go do what it takes, within the rules, to win!"

Zuya and Wétu get the Lakota High girls to stand and huddle. Grabbing hands in the air, they shout together, "What it takes!"

When Lakota runs back into their gym, the Nation is ready and roaring. Wétu notices on the sideline all three referees in a huddle, including the native-looking woman. They are having a meeting before the half with Aberdeen coaches, and MacDonahough too.

THIRD QUARTER: Condors 35 — Marmots 55

Aberdeen Condors got a new system. They used their ten minutes. Shut down Lakota's scoring machine—slow down the game. Aberdeen defense challenges quicker, guards closer, takes advantage of weak post, forces Marmot's to throw the ball backwards. Aberdeen offense don't play three-point catchup, play for shots under the net. They stop getting tired.

But do they got something else? Wétu thinks. *Do they got the refs?* Now refs say every Lakota hand's a reaching, pushing foul machine. Lakota charging from a mile away and muscly white girls go tumbling like bowling pins. Refs put wasicus back in the game, ticky tack fouls and free throws. Meanwhile, Condors grab Marmot jerseys like they're going to steal them.

Wétu stuffs a Condor layup, a play on the ball she did all first half, all season. The Condor crashes and the ref gives Wétu an "unsportspersonlike." Coach Proudhorse has to bench her, Wétu's two from fouling out. *If this was WNBA they'd let me have six.* It's their plan—pick on Brings Water, put her under pressure to make mistakes. Lakota Nation don't like it, they let everybody hear it and the refs threaten technical fouls on Nation.

Wétu's on the bench watching Lakota's lead slip away. She's got minutes to think. Like how a hundred years ago, did Coach Proudhorse say, this east-coast white man claimed basketball, wrote a rulebook. The ball and the basket, dribble only but never double dribble, no contact. Rulebook is leagues, fifteen-girls in uniforms, refs, lines on all sides of the court and down the middle, the three-point arc and the free throw lane, and a lot of words about what's fair. *The rulebook tells peeps what's basketball, and not volleyball or Monopoly; the lines tell everybody what to do, even though they ain't nothing but paint.* When Wétu was a kid her uncles taught her basketball rules on half-court asphalt lines outside. But they never showed her any book that said don't hold the ball and run to the hoop, or when someone passes you the ball, don't take it and throw it down the well. She was five and she knew what to do. And it's written in the rulebook, no contact. *But if everyone on your team never fouled, you'd never win.* The bench is outside the sideline, she's not allowed to cross while the ball's in play. *There's the lines but then there's players, coaches, and refs figuring out the fair way to bend them into the final score. In basketball, the rules and the game ain't the same thing.*

Even off-rez, the law is different from how it's enforced. *Don't get Ms. Proudhorse started on U.S. law and Native Americans.* In basketball the written rule's no contact—the game is contact. Call it unwritten rules. *Like an unwritten language*, Wétu thinks. *And each game's the ref's interpretation.* It's not about players getting away with fouls or what refs don't see. Refs expect fouls, every team tries. *Some fouls hurt your team, some fouls win games.* Refs are the police of the written rules, which they allow to be broken for fair reasons. Nobody calls playing by unwritten rules cheating. *Coach Proudhorse calls it "gamespersonship."*

FORTH QUARTER: Condors 66 — Marmots 60

Lakota is losing. Coach Proudhorse has to risk Wétu back in the game. Lakota girls got to be better gamespersons than the refs and find smarter points fast.

Lakota players race Aberdeen's to a spot, make their offense charge so refs have to give Lakota possession. Lakota steals in the passing lane, streaks all the way to the hoop. They pressure in-bounds passes, force turnovers. Mostly, they make Aberdeen foul—stick the ball out to draw reaches, pump fake shots, shoot off both feet to get knocked over.

Seconds on the clock, Lakota down four points. Wétu inbound from the baseline to Zuya, who has clear-court dribble to the three-point line, defenders are waiting. Zuya pass back to Wétu running behind her. Wétu with a jumper three outside the line, ball flies over Condors into the hoop. Lakota down by two. A Marmot tries to pick up a rebound from the floor, ball's knocked out. Condors get an inbound under the basket. Throw arcs out to MacDonahough at the high post, but Wétu gets her hand in front. On one foot she pulls the ball in, shifts to her back foot, angles toward Lakota's net. MacDonahough plays for the ball in the middle of Brings Water's acrobatics. Wétu heaves the ball from one hand, final tenths of a second, a prayer comes down through the net with the final buzzer. Condors think there's overtime but the ref, the one Wétu thinks is native, blows the whistle. Personal foul—MacDonahough. Aberdeen tries to argue no contact, but the ref's call stands. Wétu's tied the game and drawn an after-regulation foul shot.

Both teams make regulation lines along the free throw lane. Wétu sinks the and-one. Lakota High wins by one point.

FINAL: Condors 81 — Marmots 82

Lakota advances to semis. Wétu rides on the shoulders of her team, Nation parties in the rafters. Even Unci stands up. But Wétu feels stuck on that last second of regulation.

Ref whistled foul, Wétu knows MacDonahough never touched her. Maybe it looked foul from the ref's angle. Is that ref native, did she cheat, put Lakota back in the game? Whatever her angle, the ref, not the wasicu man's own rulebook, decided the winner. Because the ref's human. They cheat, call cheap fouls, overuse the book, make up new rules if the book don't say. They got emotions, and agendas, maybe some don't like a gym full of loud brown people. But sometimes a bad call's just a bad call, a mistake. They make a decision about what they think they saw even if what happened is different.

Wétu's not sure. *Even if the white people were cheating, ain't I cheating to know the truth and let an unwritten rule happen?* There wasn't no rule in the book to save Aberdeen. *If I'm the star of the game, it'd be fair to let the losers chop off my head.*

Cooperstown: An Insider's Guide

It's a blessing and a curse.
When I tell someone where I live,
I'm always asked if I've ever been to the Hall of Fame
I'll say No just to see their reaction, inside joke
to us townies. Out-of-state relatives and friends assume
I'll go in with them. "You're on your own," I'll say.
"Phone me when you're done." From Boston, I was born
knowing the "Curse of the Bambino," and am so glad
it's over. The blessing is that it is Cooperstown, a small,
beautiful village at the end of Otsego Lake where
the Susquehanna begins. And you could walk right past
the Hall and not know it's there. Understated, subtle,
no garish signs or lights. The curse is summer weekends
are best left entirely to baseball fans and other tourists.
Usually there's not too many, and most are polite,
bedazzled by all the souvenir shops, willing, for a price,
to engrave your name on a bat, where you can buy
a baseball cap in every incarnation of major and minor,
making it easy for us to know where you are from
or root for. "How are things in Baltimore?" I'll ask,
though I don't really care, the friendly local-color
character I'm trying hard to become, bearded, grizzled,
harmless to fish, flesh, fowl (even to some Yankee fans).
Ignored more often than not. On the day the new inductees
are ushered into the Hall, our almost-always-otherwise
peaceful village imitates a town on the Cape or Jersey Shore.
Too many fans, too many cars. A secret I hold back: a small
cement stoop and lone door, about twenty feet from the Hall's
entrance, site of the first inductee ceremony. Now they're held

at the complex about a mile out of town. Beside that door
a small brass plaque can tell you that on June 12, 1939,
Eddie Collins, Walter Johnson, Nap Lajoie, Tris Speaker,
Connie Mack, Grover Alexander, Cy Young, George Sisler,
Babe Ruth, Ty Cobb, and Honus Wagner were inducted there.
How many names do you recognize? What teams did they play for?
What positions? If you don't know the answers, I'll take you in
to see their plaques and personal items. Even blindfold me,
I could guide you because I know where they are by heart.
When I go downtown, I sit on the stoop for a while, or on the steps
of the Post Office, directly across the street, and watch people
pass by the small, eye-level plaque, telling what happened
on that day in 1939 when some of the greatest players
of all time stood there together. I'm always surprised
when someone stops to read the plaque. I won't tell them
it's there. My little secret. It's safe with you, isn't it?
Maybe I'll point it out if you come for a visit.
But don't come in summer. Most likely I'll be at home
watching the Red Sox and Yankees, who always have
something other than baseball in mind, each team more
intent on proving the other team wrong than thinking
what it takes to win the game or make it into the Hall.
If any of the players get in, come see me. I'll point you
to the entrance. It's right across the street from the Post Office.

Robert Harlow

Baseball Truth Love Time

Rick Campbell

I'm in Valdosta, Georgia, at a writer's conference and I've just finished reading a poem about Roberto Clemente when Quincy Troupe Jr. comes to sit with me. Quincy tells me that his father was a scout for the Cardinals and that he "discovered" Clemente. He also says his father was the second-best catcher in the Negro Baseball Leagues (second to Josh Gibson). Later I find his baseball card, and it's pretty good proof of that fair claim. Trouppe Sr. hit over .300 for his career and for one brief moment in 1952 played in the Major Leagues for the Cleveland Indians. I think we, white baseball fans, make too much of this—Trouppe, Paige, Monte Irvin's playing in the white leagues, as if that, and not their long great careers in the Negro League, is the truly important story. But it's too soon to digress. Quincy's story about his father led me back to my grandfather.

* * *

My grandfather said he was a "pretty good ball player." He also claimed that he was offered a contract by the Indians, but he turned it down because he was making more money working in the mill and playing semi-pro ball. Though I ignored my doubts then, as a young child, I have always found that a little hard to believe. Why would a young man in Ohio just before or soon after 1918 not take a professional contract if baseball was what he loved? Maybe there are good reasons. Maybe a lot of young men turned down contracts like these. I've always looked at this part of the claim as if I were being offered a contract, and maybe I also think of today's salaries, though I know that then my grandfather might have been offered only a few hundred dollars, if that. I look at this part of the story romantically.

After I wasn't a kid anymore, I saw some other things that could easily have influenced this matter. My grandfather was at heart a timid man, not one to take chances. He could have been someone who would turn down a chance, however slim, to play big league ball. I know that now, but I did not want to admit it then. As Quincy told me about his father, he made it impossible for me to believe my grandfather's stories, the ones most central to the good part of my childhood, without giving them serious thought and investigation.

* * *

Besides his claim about the Indians' offer, my grandfather also told me a story about how he played against Satchel Paige and Josh Gibson one afternoon at the old Idora Park ballfield in Youngstown, Ohio. He told this story, and all of his baseball stories, with all the passion and attention to setting and detail that a good storyteller brings to the tale. His exploits ranged from the pedestrian (striking out against Paige) to the fantastic (robbing Gibson of a long home run). After my conversation with Quincy, I went to the baseball encyclopedia, to the Web, and checked Paige and Gibson's birthdates. Some big disparities stared me in the face, and I had to conclude that my grandfather's stories were almost certainly not true. After my initial disappointment (maybe there is no "after," I am still disappointed), I began to wonder if my grandfather's stories were fictions or lies. That's what this essay is about—writing, not my grandfather's character and my disappointment—though both of those states entwine in this inquiry.

* * *

How do we tell fiction from lies, or, more importantly, lies from fiction? All fiction, technically, is a lie since it's not true. But is a lie fiction? Now we get into matters of intent and audience. If my grandfather had been a writer his stories would have been fiction, but since he told them to me, a little kid who loved him more than I loved my father, and loved baseball more than I loved anything else, I say these stories crossed the line from fiction to lies. I expected him to tell the truth.

* * *

Most people tell lies so that they can benefit in some manner from the lie. I wonder what my grandfather wanted and just what he got from these lies. I wonder if he told them to anyone else. From me, he got love, but not because of the stories—I already loved him. He taught me to play baseball; he taught me to play checkers. We sat in the carport summer nights and listened to Pirates games on the radio. I spent more time with my grandfather than I spent with my father. He didn't have to lie about playing against Satchel Paige to win anything from me.

* * *

I believed these stories, more or less unconditionally, for more than 50 years. Why was I worried about them now? It seems crazy, but I couldn't stop myself. I had to find out when Paige was born: 1906, give or take a couple of years. Satchel was often an unreliable narrator. Gibson was born in 1912. I did the math. I could have done it years ago, but Grandpa's baseball stories I've never had the courage to investigate. His other stories? I've strongly doubted that he was a heroic town constable, doubted that he was a charismatic union organizer, but I never let those doubts slip over into the baseball world we shared. We went to Forbes Field together. We saw my Pirate heroes—Roberto Clemente, Mazeroski, Virdon, Hoak, Skinner, Smoky Burgess, and the less heroic Dick Stuart. He told me about Pie Traynor and the Waner brothers, Big and Little Poison. He told me about Nap Lajoie, Tris Speaker, Lou Boudreau and other Cleveland Indians heroes from his childhood.

My early research revealed that my grandfather, born in 1896, was about ten years older than Paige and 16 years older than Gibson. My grandfather married in 1925. His baseball stories are always of games in Ohio, so I figure he played his baseball (if he played, I have to say now) before he married and came to our hometown of Baden, Pennsylvania. I don't remember any stories of his playing organized ball after he came to what would be my hometown. Later he coached kids' teams and Legion ball too, but I am pretty sure the mill league and Barnstorming games were much earlier in his life.

Why just pretty sure? The fragility of my memories, yes, but none of my aunts and uncles, or my father, ever said that they saw their father play baseball. No one told me anything at all about what he did those first years of his marriage. No one ever told me how he met my grandmother or why he moved to her town rather than the other way around. I guess he could have hooked up with a bunch of guys in Baden, in Beaver County to put a team together to play a Barnstorming team with Paige and Gibson on it, but there's that detail about Idora Park and Youngstown and we are back to Ohio again. A bunch of Beaver Valley mill hunks would probably play on a local field, not go to Youngstown. True, it's not that long a drive, but it was a lot longer in the Twenties than it is now.

The numbers here are a word problem. If Satchel Paige got out of Mount Meigs Negro Reform School and began playing ball for the Mobile Tigers in 1924, and my assumption that my grandfather was done playing mill league ball shortly before 1925 is accurate, in 1924, when Paige began his professional baseball career he would have been about 18, and he would have had only about a year to get on a Barnstorming team and make it from Mobile to Ohio. Barnstorming teams were made of All Stars, and Paige would have been a rookie. The odds are so small that my grandfather played against Paige, but is it impossible? Grandpa would have been 28 in 1924.

Josh Gibson presents an almost insurmountable problem; Gibson would have been about 13 when I figure my grandfather ended his playing days.

There's no way to believe Grandpa caught or chased a long fly ball off Gibson's bat at Idora Park or anywhere else. Can I say for sure that my grandfather was lying about this? I had to consider it, seriously, sadly, but I never wanted to before and I still don't like to do it now.

* * *

I suspected then, in Valdosta, that this would happen, that I would come home and look things up. My heart sank as Quincy spoke with great love and admiration about his father's baseball career. Do I still love these stories? I don't know. They are good stories, but I think I loved them because I loved my grandfather. He had no license to lie.

I do. I have a badge that says writer. If I write fiction, maybe it's based on my life, maybe not. If I write a poem in a persona, I can say I made it up. I don't try to pass fiction off as truth. I wouldn't hurt anyone or disappoint anyone just to tell a good story. If I am writing nonfiction, maybe I don't know what's true, so I say that I think this happened. I'm fascinated by the line, the world maybe, where what we imagine, desire, or experience all blend into stories that might have happened, stories that we would like to be true, lives we would like to have lived. Sometimes we believe these stories long enough, hard enough, passionately enough to make them our lives. The narratives spawn details, the settings become more than plausible, the possibilities become probable.

* * *

I'm not lying, I'm writing.

* * *

My grandfather was lying. My grandfather knew enough about baseball to populate his stories with the most dramatic of heroes, but it's not possible that these were honest mistakes. He lied. I think. Right now, I'm checking my memory, which means I'm doubting my memory. When did my grandfather tell me these stories? Where were we sitting? What were we doing? I can't remember. I can't see anything. I've been telling and writing these stories for so long, but I have no proof that he told them. Most of the time there was no one there but Grandpa and me. Grandpa and Grandma are dead. My father is dead. If my grandfather's spirit were to come back and disavow all that I think I heard, could I argue with him? Could I prove that he is wrong? If he did not tell me these stories, how do I know them? I could have made them up, and that, I guess, would be a kind of lying, since I claim that my grandfather told the stories. But I can't, for a moment, believe that I made these stories up. When I was a little kid all I knew of Paige and Gibson, Walter Johnson and the others of my grandfather's era, I heard from him. I've never seen the field at Idora Park; I don't know that the outfield would be shadowed in the late afternoon.

I don't know how fast my grandfather could run. But many sandlot fields are shadowed in the afternoon and most good centerfielders are fast. It's not hard to make up stories like these.

My grandfather's Gibson story is very specific. He claimed (I think) that it's the ninth inning, late afternoon, and the shadows are deep in centerfield. Josh Gibson is at the plate. Grandpa says that he has a ball in his back pocket. When I first wrote an essay using Grandpa's story, I claimed he said he was taking the ball home to my father, but my father was born in 1928 and now I am pretty sure Grandpa wasn't robbing Josh Gibson of a mighty hit in 1928. Maybe this is a lie within a lie. Why would my grandfather put my father, his unborn son, in the Gibson story? I guess he figured I wouldn't catch him in the lie. I guess, too, that he never told the story to my father or someone who would catch the lie. Actually, my grandfather never really cared if he was caught in these types of lies. He was just telling stories. Charlie Campbell was a bullshitter, people said, but they did not call him a liar.

My grandfather said that Gibson hit a towering shot into left center, and he got on his horse and ran deep into the gap, but he knows he's not going to catch up to the ball, so he reaches into his hip pocket and tosses the other ball into the air, then leaps, backhands it and flashes it to the ump who's still standing near second base. Ump calls Gibson out. I've written this story, in my grandfather's voice, many times. I've chronicled Gibson's shocked reaction, his brief argument with the ump. I've written it so many times that it's as much my story as Grandpa's. Maybe more mine? I'm sure I know more about Paige and Gibson than he did, sure that I can invent that ballfield at Idora Park better than he could. When I say that he ran into the gap, I see myself streaking toward the fence. When I say he leaped and backhanded the ball, I see me leaping. I know that I have made that catch once or twice and dreamed of making it countless times. I've played a thousand baseball games on dozens of fields. I'm a bit unnerved by all of this now. I've told stories about doing everything my grandfather claims to have done but playing against barnstorming Black ballplayers.

Am I telling the truth in my baseball stories, my road stories, my love stories? Do I know enough about what facts can be proven to not place a disputable fact in my fictional memoirs? Do I practice plausible deniability?

I still don't believe I made up my grandfather's baseball stories, but maybe I embellished them too much and pushed them over the line? After I found out when everyone was born, I looked on the Web for some record of Grandpa's Industrial League teams. I couldn't find any evidence. No box scores. No records of games. No mention of Charlie Campbell getting a hit, scoring a run. But that's not too unusual. If my Grandpa played Mill League ball it would have been between 1914 and 1918, and maybe again between 1919 and 1924. The war would have dominated the news then. The Industrial Leagues probably did not keep good records and the newspaper morgues from small Ohio towns a hundred years or so ago are unlikely to be stored on the internet.

When I google my grandfather there's no record of him. No obituary, nothing at all. He lived, but there's little evidence of his life. Children, grandchildren, stories, but whose? I wrote to my grandfather's children, my aunts and my uncle, and asked them if they had heard any of these baseball stories. They said no, but they had little interest in baseball. And though they did not tell me this—they did not have much interest in their father's life either. I've never heard them talk about anything that he did. I am following the Campbell tradition. I know next to nothing about my father's family and what I do know is from my own experience (or perhaps my imagination?). No one can bail me out of this.

* * *

I love the idea that my grandfather was a good enough ballplayer to strike out against Satchel Paige and rob Josh Gibson of a home run. I've loved the idea long enough to want to believe it. Do I love it enough to still believe it now that I'm almost certain it never happened? Next question—do I love it enough to have made it up and then believe that I didn't? I hope not. That sounds sort of borderline psycho-something. I don't believe my grandfather played against Paige or Gibson, but I don't know who made the story up.

Even now, long years after his death, it's important to me to believe he could play ball. He does not have to be as good as he claimed he was. It's ok if he embellished his skills a little; I've done that too. Maybe I wasn't as great a shortstop back in 1968 as I've told a lot of people I was, but I believe I was as good as I think I was. I want Grandpa to be that kind of good.

If I've made up my "Grandpa's baseball stories," woven out of whole cloth, I'm going to be shocked. It's going to shake the foundations of what I think I remember and blur what happened with what did not. If I made them up before I was a writer, then I was a liar; but since they are good stories, I believe I could not have created them until I was a writer. If I made up the stories and attributed them to my grandfather so that I could write a good story, then I can forgive myself for that.

But if I made up these stories that were so important to my life, what would I not make up in order to tell a good story? I'm afraid I'm going to doubt most of my memories, especially the ones fueled by my desires. What if I want something to be true that isn't? What will I remember?

* * *

Theory

The intersection of memory and desire is not the boundary of memory and desire. To say that memory and desire intersect is to conjure the image of streets, crossroads, lines of force and energy flowing or moving through some other field or world, call it space, time, life. Memory and desire would be in that world but separate from it. The boundary of memory and desire tells us that memory and desire are lands, countries, maybe worlds that border each other. One can see where memory and desire might share a border as porous as all boundaries, a river meandering, sometimes into memory, sometimes into desire. Sometimes the river floods and memory and desire mingle. And always, even in their most stable state, memory and desire share the river, meet in the middle like Illinois meets Iowa, or Ohio meets Kentucky. Sometimes the river slows and widens and becomes a lake. Memory and desire flow together and the banks of each recede in distance and fog.

On the boundary of memory and desire is where we live. Sometimes we live more in the land of memory, sometimes more in the land of desire. Maybe in the land of desire, time, the motion of our thoughts, moves forward into what might be, rather than backwards toward what was. Memory is the land of what was, or at least the land of what we think happened. But the border is porous. Memory and desire overlap, embrace, create, or in some more subtle manner, influence each other. Desire summons memory. Memory kindles desire. Desire rewrites memory. Memory erupts into desire.

Like this—there's this story, but I can't remember its provenance. The centerfield fence in old Forbes Field was so deep, 465 feet, that the grounds crew kept the batting cage out there on the playing field. Someone hit a long shot to center and Billy Virdon raced back, climbed the cage, and caught the ball. The story might be true. I tried to look it up, but even if I found no record of it, it still might have happened. Sometimes when I tell the story of this play, I do it in a way that does not exclude my having been there, my having seen it. Sometimes I clearly state that I just heard the story. When do I allow people to think that I saw it? Usually in a bar with other baseball storytellers.

* * *

Quincy Troupe's father is in the Negro Baseball Hall of Fame and the Mexican Baseball Hall of Fame too. He's even a character in Mark Winegardner's baseball novel, Veracruz Blues. Quincy has that to bank on. I'm left measuring what I think I remember against what I desire and what I have desired. I suppose, as a nonfiction writer's dilemma, it's not too bad, not really a moral problem. But if I'm a liar, if Rick Campbell is just a bullshitter, that's not something to be proud of.

At a border of memory and desire is where I am now, but it's not as adventurous as it sounds. Usually, memory and desire are more like puddings than fast flowing rivers. They just sort of hang around, but don't effect much change. They are cats rubbing against each other, not a big wind blowing through the trees. If memory and desire were always madly, passionately changing and charging each other, our lives would be too unstable. We would live, as Richard Eberhart said, "at the pitch that is near madness." No, usually we're just here, remembering something, forgetting something, desiring something; memory and desire seldom roil inside us like a flash flood and drag us away to lands we've long desired, or places we should not go. I said seldom. Sometimes they take us away and it's as if we are lost and it takes a good long while to find our way home.

Growing Up

At night my dad told stories about the professional player
he used to admire who only dribbled with his right hand,

until a reporter asked, "How come you never dribble left?"
and he said, "Because no one stops me when I go right."

Dad would laugh, then look at me dead serious.
We both knew I'd never be that good.

So every day I shot 100 left hand layups,
keeping track on a yellow piece of paper

I took with me to the gym. Now and then Dad would come too
and rebound, admonishing me to aim for the back of the rim,

get my elbow in, and to put some damn arch on my shot.
We'd end with a game of one-on-one,

me against the big man, all six foot seven of him,
mano a mano. The first time I beat him I was 12,

with a leaping-laner from the left side
that banked home soft for the win.

He'd been playing hard, and I knew it.
By the time I was 14, it was like taking candy from a baby.

There were games where I told myself
I was only going to touch the ball with my left hand

just to give him a chance, so that the game lasted
more than, say, three minutes. Twenty-one, win by four,

only I'd beat him by sixteen. All because he'd told me
that story about the dude who couldn't go left.

Dave Nielsen

Kid Ball

Adam Berlin

"The streets sound quiet here."

"They are."

"Want to take a walk?"

"I'd like that," she said.

I got out of her bed and got my clothes off the floor.

We dressed and went down.

We stayed west close to the warehouses, eighteen-wheelers parked inside the wide garages where goods got loaded and unloaded. Outside a car wash two men in overalls smoked cigarettes waiting for the next customer to pull in. I could smell the river over the exhaust smell. We were outside and we didn't take each other's hand. We just walked close and didn't talk much.

Anna pointed out a restaurant and asked if I'd ever eaten there. I mostly listened to her low voice.

We walked down to Canal Street, then circled back. It was hot but I didn't mind the heat and it was quiet. We passed a school playground. I walked up to the fence, put my fingers around the metal, looked in. Anna did the same next to me. I could feel her body almost touching mine. A bunch of kids were playing a pick-up game of baseball. They didn't wear uniforms and there were no umpires or coaches around. Just a game where they used regular bats and a tennis ball instead of a hard ball.

The kid at bat hit a grounder and ran. The play at first was close.

The kids started screaming, arguing whether the kid on first had been safe or out. The kid on first kept both his feet on the base like that was going to prove he was safe. The other kids kept screaming and recreating the play. I leaned against the fence. The metal links were hot from the sun.

Finally, they let the kid stay on first. The next batter missed two pitches before he hit the tennis ball weakly to second. The kid at second gloved the ball and stepped on the base forcing the runner out. The teams switched places. Some of the kids exchanged gloves as they ran past each other. The pitcher warmed up with the tennis ball. The catcher kept throwing the ball back short. One of the first things a catcher learns is to get the ball back to the pitcher quickly and accurately. You don't want the pitcher working any more than he has to. It's the catcher's job to keep the pitcher rested, to keep him calm, to keep him focused on the game. I'd been good at that. Defense had been the best part of my game.

The pitcher yelled batter up. The kids in the infield started their chatter. No batter, no batter. Strike him out. Come on, come on. It didn't seem to matter to these kids that they were playing on blacktop when the game was meant to be played on grass, that the bases weren't proper bases but only squares painted on blacktop. I stayed where I was and watched the next kid come to the plate. He looked more serious than the others and held his bat confidently but without making a show of it. He kept his back arm straight the way you're supposed to. He drove the first pitch over the left fielder's head and rounded the painted bases with a smooth stride and came home easily while the kids bobbled the ball in the field. His teammates surrounded him and congratulated him. He looked like he was used to being the center of attention. He was a good-looking kid and if he stuck with it he'd make the school team if the school had a team and maybe more. He was a good-looking kid and if things didn't work out, he'd find something. The pitcher held the tennis ball until the little celebration was over and started to pitch to the next batter.

She was quiet next to me. Just watching the kids. Maybe she was coming up with something to write about or maybe she didn't need to use the scene for anything else. She had nice hands. Her skin was dark and looked warm against the links of the fence and she was really watching the kids.

"He's good," I said.

"He is. Cute kid."

"He is."

"My grandfather was a big fan. I mean he used to be. He didn't like the way baseball went with the free agents and how there didn't seem to be any allegiance to the teams. He was a big Brooklyn Dodgers fan. It broke his heart when they moved to California. Jackie Robinson. Pee Wee Reese. I remember him saying those names. Duke Snider. Roy Campanella."

"He was a great catcher. At least that's what I've read."

The sound of tennis ball against bat made me turn and I watched a kid run to first and beat the throw.

"Safe," I said.

The kids didn't hear me. There wasn't much of an argument.

"I take it you're from the city."

"Born and bred."

"Brooklyn?"

"My mom and dad were," she said. "They moved to Manhattan when they got married. I grew up in the city."

"One of those Manhattan kids. I always wonder about them. They seem old before their time."

"I was pretty sheltered as a kid."

"That's good."

"I think so."

"The Brooklyn Dodgers."

"I never really followed baseball," she said. "My poor dad had no one to talk sports with. What about you?"

"I used to talk baseball all the time."

"Like these kids."

"I'd bet more than these kids."

"Were you a good player?"

"I was. I played ball for a while. Minor league ball."

"Really?"

"Really."

"Where did you play?"

"Salt Lake City. They have a Triple A team there. The Salt Lake Bees. I'm sure you've never heard of them. You know the Los Angeles Angels?"

"I've heard of them."

"That's their minor league team."

"I've never met anyone who played ball for a living."

"It wasn't much of a living. It was fun for a while though. There were moments I felt that was the place I most wanted to be."

The kids on the blacktop switched sides. Some of the kids coming in switched gloves with the kids going out.

"It must be rough not playing on grass," I said.

"Manhattan kids. They seem to be managing."

The pitcher warmed up with a few throws to the catcher. The good-looking kid was at first base. That was a smart place to be. A safe position. No foul tips coming at you. No spikes. No walls to crash into chasing fouls. I hadn't really talked baseball with anyone for a while. Not my baseball career. It felt like too long ago and the reactions I got were almost always the same. False encouraging words. Too many questions. What name players I'd seen moving up. I knew she wouldn't push, so I offered. I felt like talking about baseball, so I did. It felt good just standing there and talking with her listening, her body almost touching mine, her fingers through the fence dark and warm, the two of us looking at the kids playing ball.

"The Bees. We were a pretty good team. Or they used to be. I don't keep up with them now that I'm gone."

"What position did you play?"

"I caught. I was a catcher."

"That always seemed like a hard position. Like they're always in the way of danger. They're the only ones with all that padding."

"I liked it. A catcher sees the whole picture."

"The whole picture or the big picture?"

"Pretend this fence is a catcher's mask and that you're just a few feet closer to the plate and you can get the feeling of what it's like. You see the ball coming in. You see the kid swinging and missing the pitch. You see all the positions in front of you. The faces of all your teammates waiting to spring into action if the ball gets hit. It makes you feel like you're in control of the game."

"Are you?"

"Do you feel in control right now?"

"Not really."

"Now you know the truth about catching. But if you were behind the plate and your team was depending on you, you'd pretend you were. That's part of the catcher's game face. You'd know the hitters. You'd know your pitcher. You'd do your best to make yourself feel in control. Or as in control as you can be."

A kid hit a grounder to second. The second baseman picked it up and threw to first. The good-looking kid at first took the throw and started throwing the ball around the horn.

"He's good," I said.

"Were you?"

"That's a bold question."

"I'm curious."

"I was good enough to make Triple A. Not good enough to make the big league."

"Do you miss it?"

"Sometimes."

"Do you miss it now?"

"Right now?"

"Right now."

Her voice was low when she said it and she was looking at me and we were almost touching. I'd see the wind-up and follow the ball in and frame the pitch and wait for the call behind me. And there was everyone and everything in front of me.

"Right now, I'm looking at you."

"I'm glad," she said.

"Good."

There was the sound of tennis ball against bat, but I didn't turn to see the action. I heard sneakers on blacktop and the sound of ball hitting glove.

"I've seen enough baseball for the day," I said.

I took my hands from the fence and she did the same and we started to walk, not touching but close, and it was hot and there was hardly anyone on the street and it looked like the city kept going and going but it didn't.

King of the Hill

Mr. Ryan
Looking in, ornery intentional
Hits that kid square (and he knew it)
The fool runs up the bump to get his due
But he's flapping his arms like the sandhill crane mating game
The Texan headlocks him and bashes fist into mouth
Crunch one crunch two, six times rapidly pounding
Before the benches flow up to stir oil and water
And, I expect, gushing blood
What bullfight excitement!

An American Man
All by the rules.

E. Martin Pedersen

[Author's note: Twenty years after writing this, I looked it up. The batter was Robin Ventura of the White Sox. The incident happened at Arlington Stadium on August 4, 1993.]

Being Waved Around

Bob Carlton

Ulysses Adams could still remember the day he knew that his major league dreams would never come true. Ricky Fortunata had been pitching for the opponent, and he was starting to tire a bit by the third inning. His fastball, never an overpowering weapon to begin with, was coming in straight, and Ricky was starting to aim it to keep it over the plate. Ulysses had gotten the count in his favor at three and one, and so knew what was coming and where it would be. No better pitch to hit had ever been created, and Ulysses did not miss it. He had never felt a ball hit a bat like this before as he let every bit of potential energy uncoil its way through his body and into the pitch. It was the most perfect moment he had ever known at the plate, and he watched for a split second as the ball shot toward center field. He sprinted toward first, fully expecting to slow to a trot as he headed into second base, maintaining a triumphant, yet respectful pace as he made his way home. As the ball hopped its way back to the infield, he found himself standing, amid a smattering of cheers and applause from the bleachers, at third base, winded and a little bewildered at how it was possible that his hit did not clear the fence. When, at the end of that season, Ulysses had made the all-star team, he suspected it was the last such moment he was likely to have.

So here he was, a year later, with the winning run at second and no outs. Before him lay a nine-headed monster, wounded but still deadly, and the club he carried was not big enough to kill it with one blow. Ulysses knew the role of hero was not his to play. He also knew that physical excellence can take more than one form, that brute power is not the only weapon that can vanquish an enemy. Some are meant to fall in battle; the key was not to fall in vain. Ever since coming to the realization of his own baseball mortality, Ulysses Adams had become a smarter ballplayer. He knew the opposing pitcher threw hard. He knew that he could not pull the ball. But sometimes, a player's strength can be his weakness and vice versa. Ulysses swung at the first pitch and hit a weak ground ball to first, moving the runner to third base. The next day, no one would remember that it was Ulysses Adams who put him there, only that Chance Kearnes crushed a walk off home run to the deepest part of the park in left-center, the ball lost in the thick stand of trees where no one had ever put a baseball before. In the jubilation of victory, Ulysses himself forgot that his own act of self-denial had been rendered meaningless. Everyone gathers at home plate when the winning run scores.

* * *

Ulysses knew of many players who made up for physical shortcomings through being smart, by knowing the game better than their opponents. He knew he was never going to be a great ballplayer, he was never going to be the popular kid who dated the prom queen; he was even smart enough to know he wasn't the smartest. But what he did know might keep him in the game. Watching Game of the Week on TV, he came to appreciate what a pitcher was doing by throwing over to first. What a bad pick-off move, he would think. The crowd would get anxious after a couple of tosses, and if it was a visiting pitcher, they would quickly begin booing. But Ulysses began to understand. Obviously, the pitcher was trying to keep the runner close; everyone knew that. But he was also showing a particular move, one the runner would see over and over, one he could get used to and time. It would all become routine and annoying, especially to the spectators, until the perfect moment, when all would be revealed, and death would cut down those who did not pay attention.

As the season wore on, as he played less and less, Ulysses knew that this summer would be the last he would spend on a regulation diamond. He had already sensed his body would not develop into that of an athlete, that for him, the game that defined his day and made meaningful his life, would become a game played only in the mind. The less he played, the more he saw the unfolding story, not so much a competitive sport at which he no longer excelled, but a dramatic ritual, the action shaping a series of constantly changing constellations enacting the same old tales with seemingly infinite variations. Guessing pitch sequences, stealing signs, knowing which base to throw to given the flux of events: all this and more he knew he would know better than most who play past childhood, better than those with the physical gifts to continue. No matter how little he might play, he would still have this game available in memory and imagination, a place he could go to let the fog of his uncertainty clear, to let the sun shine down on the hard green truths, and for a moment feel sure of his world.

* * *

Among the new confusions that summer, Ulysses had suddenly become aware of certain feelings he could not, as yet, articulate very well, but which centered on Darwin Luck's sister, Moira. It was the first impossible crush of adolescence, a secret longing, his unformed desires directed at a girl two years older, immensely popular, and a beauty nonpareil. The fact that this could have described the situation of any number of his peers did not lessen his feelings of isolation or pubescent despair in the least. That Moira no doubt had the tacit knowledge of her powers, the awareness of exciting desires without the possibility of fulfillment, confirmed her as the exemplar of evil in the world. Yet Ulysses longed on. So complete were his reveries of an unachievable bliss and almost unbearable present agony that he was half way to the park before he heard any of the words Chance had been saying to him.

"...and Ricky says he's been working on his curveball. Might waste one ahead in the count."

"Hmph," snorted Ulysses, "like it would make a difference to me anymore."

Ulysses had known Chance Kearnes most of his life. Chance was the kid everyone knew was going to be in the big leagues one day. Not only was he a marvelous athlete, but he was gifted with that special baseball intellect that allows the full expression of ability in action. It was the pre-conscious neural reasoning that would cause a twelve-year-old to take three steps over and four more in from his normal position in center field toward the gap in left when a left-handed hitter would foul a two-oh fastball into the bleachers along the third base line. No one but Ulysses, sitting on the bench, noticed. When the batter hacked at the next pitch, floating a soft line drive into shallow left-center, Chance loped over in a few easy steps and made the catch. Ulysses was beginning to realize how difficult it might be to gauge a player's true greatness. All those acrobatic, diving catches on the TV highlights: were they the result of superior athletic prowess, or of being out of position and getting a bad jump? Perhaps, thought Ulysses, what we see as the routine play is in reality the exceptional one, one rendered transparent because executed with efficiency and a minimal expenditure of energy by the truly transcendent player.

"Don't you worry," Chance said, "you know more about how to play this game than most big league managers. You'll do just fine."

"Yeah," chimed in Chance's little sister, Penny, "I think you're great. Better than Chance even."

She giggled at this and gave Ulysses a friendly punch on the arm. Until now, Ulysses had not even been aware of her presence, though she walked with them to almost every game. Ulysses gave her a half-hearted "thanks" and turned back to talk to Chance about the finer points of the upcoming battle. When he thought of Penny Kearnes at all, Ulysses found her harmlessly annoying, though her obvious infatuation with him had always left him bewildered and unaccountably uncomfortable. He felt he had better things to do with his time than put up with the irritating baby sister of his buddy. The more he tried to ignore her, however, the more insistent her intrusions became.

* * *

While the evolving landscape of his summer had left Ulysses with fewer and fewer certainties, there were some definite truths to which he could turn for solid footing in the world. One was that Darwin Luck was a jerk. Like most small town baseball gods, Darwin played many positions, all of them well. What bothered Ulysses was the arrogance, the way Darwin could be so cocky about his own abilities, even though they were untested anywhere out in the world. It bothered Ulysses that it would never occur to Darwin that that world was filled with small towns, each with its own version of Darwin Luck. Ulysses harbored the secret fantasy that someday, many years hence, he could return to this place in all his success and find Darwin, teenage exploits forgotten by all but himself, toiling away in obscurity like all the rest of his family.

"Here comes strike three!" Darwin drawled as he went into his wind-up, almost laughing even as he delivered the pitch. The ball came across the heart of the plate, and Ulysses let it pass, thinking it was low.

"Strike three!" yelled the umpire, as Darwin and his teammates jogged gleefully off the field, and the two runners Ulysses had left to die so far from home walked dejectedly back to the dugout.

"How is that a strike?" mumbled Ulysses, almost on the point of tears. "That was the same pitch you called a ball the pitch before."

Ulysses walked away, expecting no answer, receiving no answer. All he heard were the stupid noises and idiotic taunts of Darwin Luck. His first inning plate appearance over, Ulysses went to take his place on the bench, the conscience of Coach Posey assuaged by the knowledge that he had now early on made sure that everyone had gotten a chance to play. Ulysses shot a glance out to the parking lot beyond the chain link fence along the first base side and was both mortified and thrilled to see a group of older girls, Moira Luck among them. He prayed that she had not seen his failure at the hands of her brother. As he watched her talking to her friends, she tossed her hair and laughed, and Ulysses, in all the discomfort of his age, could simultaneously imagine her laughing at a brilliant witticism of his even while cackling with cruelty at his athletic ineptitude. A dull ache settled in his stomach, and he turned away to sulk unnoticed at the end of the bench, his day done.

* * *

If the disruptive nature of the season were not already apparent to him, his mother's announcement at dinner that evening would certainly clarify the matter.

"I talked to your father today," she said in an off-handed manner that was decidedly rehearsed. The content of the message and the form in which it arrived was enough to give Ulysses pause in the midst of chewing his peas: his mother was sending him north to stay with his father for the last two weeks of the summer before school started.

"But Mom," Ulysses protested, "baseball season's not even over yet."

His pleas fell on deaf ears. At the end of the week, he would be heading to a suburb in northern Virginia, just outside of Washington D.C., banished, he felt, a thousand miles from home into the care of a man he felt he no longer knew.

Larry Adams had been his son's hero growing up, a man of clever devices and skillful hands. Or so Ulysses had believed until three years ago, when his mother's pain and rage finally mellowed into a sustained bitterness, and divorce soon followed. Too young to understand the complexities of frail economies and imprecise ambition, Ulysses saw his father cut down from divine stature to the size of mortal shame. The once great man was revealed to be a tinkerer of no great dexterity, a thinker without a usable thought, a bumbling and hapless man who could no longer retain a decent job, his wife's respect, or his son's admiration.

The night before his departure, Ulysses went to his room after dinner to pack. Two weeks. It felt to him more like moving away forever. As he looked through all of his things, it became less a matter of deciding what he needed to bring with him, than of what must be left behind. He sorted and resorted the baseball cards spread across the bed. He had heard adults say many times in referring to themselves that they were not merely names on a piece of paper, they were not numbers, but that they were human beings. Ulysses, however, wanted nothing more right now than to be a name, to be only numbers, to be known whole and transparent at a glance, his entire life a baseball card for all to see, his name, birth date, height, weight, and accomplishments on display in orderly columns of numbers. Such a life would, of course, have to be worthy of such documentation, would have to be, if not heroic, at least honorable in order to withstand the scrutiny, the discerning discrimination of the most astute card collector.

Ulysses picked up a book, flipped through the pages, then discarded it in favor of another. He thought through the lessons he had found in them, hoping to find a clue, some guiding principle that would help make the life outside the foul lines and beyond the horizon, if not comprehensible, at least navigable. Sherlock Holmes had taught him that though there were indeed dark forces at work in the world, a man could, through the power of his mind alone, prevail against them. John Carter and Tarzan made this world, and several others, a place of high adventure that rewarded physical wit and boldness. All these men would, Ulysses believed, have formed the core of a very good baseball team.

While Ulysses showered, his mother went into his bedroom to check on his progress packing. She found, in the small suitcase that lay open on the bed, a half-dozen books by Edgar Rice Burroughs and Sir Arthur Conan Doyle, along with a baseball, a cap, and a mitt. Sighing, she gathered his clothes and toiletries and put them in the case. When Ulysses walked in a few minutes later, he found his mother sitting on his bed with his mitt on her hand, two silent tears slowly wandering down through the creases in her cheeks.

* * *

The long days, hot and humid, were at first a misery to Ulysses. He wandered the indiscriminate neighborhood, lost sometimes and not caring, since every street, every house, every human being looked the same to him. Then one day he finally got to the bottom of his suitcase and found the cap, ball, and glove that had been waiting for him there, waiting for him to find them, recognize them, reclaim them as his own. With a reluctantly accepted thrill, he donned his gear and armed himself. In his father's backyard stood an old shed, against the side of which he casually tossed the ball. It bounded back, hopping and rolling through the grass to return to rest finally with a warm familiarity in the pocket of the well-worn glove. Minutes became hours as muscles warmed to a task half-forgotten. Cheers began to crowd his ears with every cleanly executed play, invisible batters swung with bewildered impotence at the vast assortment of his pitches. When Larry Adams returned that evening from work, he found his son sitting at the kitchen table, flushed face smiling for once. The days went by, passing, if not in happiness, then at least with the contentment of a repetitive routine pleasantly mastered.

One day, as Ulysses practiced against the shed, he saw, beneath a red cap, a pair of eyes peeking over the fence along the alley. Ulysses began by ignoring them, then found himself glancing over more and more frequently. The eyes under the cap never moved. Finally, he stopped throwing the ball, turned to face the eyes, and addressed them.

"Hey," was all he said, his tone neutral, neither friendly nor defensive.

"Hey," came the reply, in a voice much like his own in both tone and age. "What you doing?"

Ulysses shrugged. "Just tossing a ball around."

"Want to play catch?" the voice of the eyes asked, containing within it the glimmer of a quickening hope.

Ulysses shrugged again. "Sure, I guess. Got a mitt?"

"Yeah," the voice replied with undisguised enthusiasm at the prospect.

"Come on around," Ulysses said.

"Name's Tommy," the boy said as he walked into the back yard and stuck out his hand.

"Ulysses," Ulysses said, matching the other boy's unexpected cordiality with a reciprocal hand of his own.

Ulysses was delighted to see that Tommy carried a genuine catcher's mitt. The rest of that day, and all those that followed, Ulysses and Tommy played catch in the back yard, taking turns as pitcher and catcher, one firing unhittable pitches as the other received them, calling balls and strikes and keeping up a running narrative of the game action.

"Heading back home tomorrow," Ulysses said one day as they were warming up, lazy throws borne along high arcs on the buzzing of cicadas.

"Be back next year you think?" Tommy asked.

"I don't know. Probably so though, I imagine."

"I'll be around," Tommy said, going into a crouch and pounding the center of the big round mitt.

* * *

His first evening back, Ulysses took a long walk alone, out to the vacant lot near the elementary school, where he and his childhood friends had played. He stood at the traditional location of home plate. There was no back stop, no well-defined diamond, only basepaths worn into the field by custom. He looked out to where the outfielders would stand, their exact positions determined only by the power of the batter, without any regard for fences or foul lines, a field that, in theory, could go on forever. It was still possible for Ulysses to be a hero in the pick-up games played here. A fly ball into that infinite outfield that went uncaught could venture into the sea of uncut grass and swim away until, spent with fatigue, it could hide in silence, sinking into the deep green waves, as Ulysses sprinted around the makeshift bases to find his way home in triumph. While former peers like Ricky, Chance, and Darwin, wearing clean uniforms, playing on a pampered field, under lights and in front of spectators, put their contained excellence on display, the athletic outcasts, Ulysses among them, could play in this uneven pasture, as long as daylight lasted and they could still see the ball as it gathered its brown and green stains. Everyone knew the score, no one counted the innings, and joy never diminished.

* * *

Epilogue

As summer turned to autumn and the slow rhythms of the playful season quickened into the hectic pace of the beginning school year, Ulysses began to feel he was where he belonged once more. As if in confirmation, one day he noticed that, suddenly, little Penny Kearnes wasn't so little anymore. At that moment, the baseball fate of the rest of his companions no longer seemed so important. When, ten years later, they were finally married, immediately after the bride and groom kissed, she whispered in his ear, "I always knew you would come home to me."

With Baseball, It's Always Spring

Old age has its advantages.
One is the full right and privilege
of playing fast and loose with the truth.
You know, those stories
about walking two miles to school
in all that ice and snow,
and those HUGE fish you caught,
and that night you met Elvis.

Mine have to do with baseball.
The older I get, the better player I become.
In another few years I'll be an All-American.
I'm aided and abetted by a nephew
who swears I was the best baseball player
in the family. And that from a man
whose two sons played college ball
and whose grandson, only a high school junior,
has already been awarded a scholarship
to play for Ole Miss.

Still, here's the story David tells,
and I gladly accept it as gospel.
As a young boy he sat in the bleachers
with my father, his grandfather,
and they both leaped to their feet and cheered
when I hit a mammoth home run
in the Mississippi State All-Star Game.

Now, to my knowledge,
there was no state all-star game in my day,
and had there been, I probably wouldn't
have been invited to play in it.
Moreover, while it's true
that I hit more than a few home runs,
I doubt that any of them
would be ranked as "mammoth."

But I suppose to a seven-year-old boy,
any game and home run you viewed
with the man you loved more than any
except your own father
might be considered heroic.

There is a kind of truth to be found
in the myths we construct and live by.
Sometimes there's more certainty
in fiction than in fact.
I never played catch with my father.
An older man who had a fourth-grade education
and who worked six days a week
at a poor-paying job to support his family,
he seldom had time to attend the games
I played and occasionally starred in.
But in the ways that really counted
he was always there for me,
and David is right to misremember him
as seated in those bleachers in that long-ago summer,
watching me play and cheering me on.

Robert Hamblin

A Place Beyond Words

Tadhg Coakley

I can't write without a reader. It's precisely like a kiss—you can't do it alone.
—John Cheever

At the Cork World Book Fest in 2019 I asked the novelist Salley Vickers why she writes and why we all read. What was compelling everyone present in the room that day towards literature in the first place? In reality, I was not so much asking about her compulsion to write—what I wanted to learn about was my own compulsion.

Salley Vickers gave an answer I will never forget. She said that we write and we read so as not to feel alone. And the reason I will never forget her answer is because I have, for a long time, felt the same way.

I also think this is why we engage with sport. When we begin to play sport, we want to be part of a collective—a community. And when we become sports fans, again we are becoming part of a community—we belong.

I recently read about an interview with David Byrne (of Talking Heads) by Olivia Laing. She asked him what music was for, what its purpose was. And he replied that music connects people. I think this is the purpose of sport, too.

And we want these connections. Connections with our past selves and those who came before us; connections with our friends and neighbors, the ties that bind us as communities; connections with our rivals and those against whom we play and pretend to hate, but secretly love.

But it goes beyond that. We also want, as players, to perform—to act. The young player wants to play, she is drawn to it—compelled to it. Sport calls young people to itself, as a vocation. When we meet that vocation, the rightness of it is almost overwhelming. And moments in our sport will provide us with an intensity of feeling that we rarely get outside it.

* * *

I have a fuzzy memory of my brother Dermot winning an All-Ireland hurling medal in September 1971. I watched it on TV in my suburban home in a small town in Ireland. I was ten years old. My memory is of running out of the house into a nearby housing estate. And Paul Redmond, my friend, was running up towards me. We met about halfway.

We didn't hug or anything. We probably just said "He did it!" or "We did it!" or talked about the game. I mostly remember my compulsion to share the moment of ecstasy with somebody else. My body could not contain the emotions I was feeling. In the same way we want to share the best movie we've ever seen or the best song we've ever heard. In the sharing, the emotion is amplified and vindicated and released.

In her book *Big Magic*, Elizabeth Gilbert writes about the moment of inspiration for a writer or artist. Once, when she was inspired by an idea for a novel, the reaction was not mental or intellectual, it was physical: "… chills ran up my arms. The hairs on the back of my neck stood up for an instant, and I felt a little sick, a little dizzy. I felt like I was falling in love, or had just heard alarming news, or was looking over a precipice at something beautiful and mesmerizing, but dangerous."

And this is a very good description of the reaction to a deep sporting moment—either as a player or supporter. The rightness of feeling is so intense as to be physical, overpowering. Empowering, too, but also difficult for our bodies to manage, to contain.

* * *

Playing is a form of asserting identity. When I was young I devised a soccer game to play around my house. It was a solo game and the idea was for me to kick the ball around the house in the least possible number of touches. I played it relentlessly.

The way that I played my game was unique to me. In fact, the very concept of the game—a game I "invented"—was unique to me. All players are different and unique. The way each of us plays is different and distinctive to who we are—just as the way every artist creates her art is unique.

Play, like art, is a form of self-expression. Deep down, every author, painter, dancer, musician, sculptor is expressing themselves and saying who they are. Artists are—through their art—saying where they come from, what they want, what they think about love, life and the universe.

What about every child who picks up a tennis racket, or kicks a ball, or wants to swim? When they are playing these games—especially when they come to compete—they too are saying where they are from, who they are, what they desire, what they think about love, life and the universe.

When a child goes down to the local soccer pitch and plays with her peers she is entering a social contract. She is saying: this is me; this is who I am; this is my mother and father, this is my family. When she represents her club, the child is saying: this is me; this is where I am from; these are my values; this is my community; this is my culture; and this is how I express it in my unique and precious way beside my friends.

She is saying: all this has value, it is my essence, my world, and I assert it. Her play is an affirmation of who she is and of the human spirit itself—just as valid and just as moving an affirmation as that proclaimed by James Joyce in his literature.

* * *

But the playing and the taking part in the games isn't enough. For the player and the artist there must be more. The player and the artist also have to be seen. If I, as a writer, want to say something, I also want others to hear it. I want people to read my books, to engage with them. Otherwise my writing becomes a hobby, something looking inward, a conversation with myself and not with the world.

Likewise, the player. If the young boxer wants to express her pride in her community, in its culture, and who she is, she also wants others to hear this expression, to know what she is saying. To listen. The listener is the fan—the person who goes to games to experience the players expressing themselves.

The fan is the writer's reader and without readers, there would be no writing. Without those who are moved by art there would be no art. There would be no point in Vincent Van Gogh or Emily Dickinson or Franz Kafka creating their art—in saying what they want to say—if nobody was listening.

Sport is a performative art. It happens live, unlike, for example, a painting by Vermeer. And the need to be seen to perform—to perform according to the mysterious will of the audience, as Joyce Carol Oates puts it—is part of the play, too.

Ultimately, when I was a child kicking my ball around my house, I was preparing for a time when I would play in teams in public. I was honing a craft that I would need when I began to play—for my hometown, Mallow, to begin with, and later for my school, my county, and my university—I knew people would be there, watching. If nobody else came to the game, at least the opposition players and my teammates and the coaches would be there watching me.

Players want this. We want to be seen to perform in a game. And the relationship between a player and the person watching, the fan, is mutually dependent. Sport wouldn't happen without fans, theatre wouldn't happen without an audience, music wouldn't happen without listeners, writing wouldn't happen without readers. Kisses, as John Cheever says, wouldn't happen without somebody to kiss.

This is art. This is sport.

* * *

The short story "Prosinečki" by Adrian Duncan was first published by the *Stinging Fly* magazine in 2018 and it's one of the great pieces of Irish sports writing. The story takes place during some stolen moments in a soccer match by an aging, journeyman professional. The player is looking back on his career and comes to the realization that his philosophy of soccer has always been erroneous—he'd been playing based on an illusory ethic of the aesthetic. He also realizes that his object of desire—to be recognized as a great pro sometime in the future in Northern England—will never happen. He has failed and he has to deal with the loss that this incurs.

The short story writer Wendy Erskine picked this story to read for the *Stinging Fly* podcast in 2019 and she did so because she saw the similarities in the story between art and football. How the story, ostensibly about football, is actually about art and how Duncan has merged the two.

Erskine and her host, the magazine's editor Danny Denton, draw out the point that, in writing, it isn't the flashy that elevates the work, but what is pragmatic, what serves the story. And this type of Dionysian or Apollonian opposition or conflict (Erskine's words) is what makes art. Erskine says that these models contrast Edgar Linton and Heathcliff, Charlie Watts and Mick Jagger, Tracey Emin and Cathy Wilkes. Very often what's beautiful in writing is what needs to be cut away. There is no beauty without purpose. And this is also true of sport.

The language in the story is not clichéd or typical of sports writing. It is measured but rich. Sport deserves this, I feel. Some examples from "Prosinečki" (interspersed, not one continuous extract):

> *When the player was young, he learned how to live a quiet life as a lesser god … When he was at his peak he could extend his personality into the opposition's shape who could not dismantle it … He could cast out nets of influence around the pitch … There was no limit to his Cartesian aptitude … His tackling was crystal … He could imagine the game three vectors ahead … He pushes the ball beyond frames of possibility.*

What Duncan is also doing is showing how articulate and intelligent athletes really are. Not in how they speak, but how they move. How they can calculate thousands of variables of time and space and act upon them. And how they can do this in milliseconds. The articulation of the intelligence of the soccer player/narrator in the story—in the *mimesis* of language and movement in the story—renders the intelligence as being true.

But just because most other athletes cannot articulate like Duncan's nameless player doesn't make them less intelligent. Their real intelligence comes from a place beyond words. In their movement we can see their expression and intelligence. But only if we look. When Sally Rooney looks at soccer, for example, she sees that "watching Mohamed Salah play football is not unlike staring up at the stars and contemplating the vastness of the universe: it makes my own life seem nice and small."

What is most impressive about "Prosinečki" is that it makes time malleable just as sport makes time malleable. The beauty of the language mirrors the beauty of the play but only in a way that furthers and deepens the story. Just as a beautiful act in soccer is beautiful only if it works, if it furthers the team's chances, so a simile is of no use without a sentence (the narrator/soccer player actually uses this image in the story).

The story is about loss, as sport is about loss. The story is about the aching urge to create perfection, just as movement in sport craves perfection. The story is about art and it is art, just as soccer and all sports are art. In art and in sport we are trying to move beyond the frames of possibility, to reach the stars and see the vastness of the universe, and Duncan achieves that in "Prosinečki."

* * *

Look at a great player: say, Serena Williams. How did she become a great player? As a child, somehow (probably to do with a parent or sibling or a peer) she was initiated into sport. She wanted to play tennis. She wanted it badly. Her motivation may have been to please her father, or to best her sister, or to prove herself to others, but whatever it was, she began to hone skills and to practice and obsess and eat, drink and sleep tennis. She watched great players, she saw the adulation they received. She saw their techniques, their fitness, their dedication. She breathed all this in and she practiced and practiced and practiced—she wanted to succeed. She exalted tennis and brushed aside the sacrifices needed to make tennis happen in her life. Then she began to play in games with others and people began to watch her and this was her object of desire. So she practiced harder. She lost games, she exposed herself in public, she got hurt. She heard the casual racism, felt the casual sexism and she plowed on. She became a great sportsperson—one of the greatest.

This is sport.

Look at a great writer: say, Edna O'Brien. How did she become a great writer? As a child, something (probably to do with a parent or sibling or a peer) led to her initiation into literature. She wanted to write. She wanted it badly. Her motivation may have been to please her mother or father, or to emulate a peer, or to prove herself to others, or to prove what women could do; but whatever it was, she began to hone skills and to practice and obsess and eat, drink and sleep books. She read the great writers, she saw the adulation they received. She hung around with writers. She saw their techniques, their style, their dedication. She breathed all this in and she practiced and practiced and practiced—she wanted to succeed. She exalted literature and brushed aside the sacrifices needed to make literature happen in her life. Then she began to send out her writing and people began to read it and this was her object of desire. So she practiced harder. Her books were rejected, they were banned. She exposed herself in public, she got hurt. She felt the casual sexism and the religious-based misogyny and she plowed on. She became a great writer—one of the greatest.

This is art.

* * *

I see so many similarities between my writing and my playing of sport. In a way, my writing is a substitute for sport and I began to write not long after I quit competitive sport.

Obviously, they are very different, physically. Physically, the art that sport comes closest to is dance. And, given I began writing only in my fifties, long after my peak sporting days, there is a huge age difference. But in so many ways, the practice and the rigor are very similar.

There is the initiation, the flicking of a switch. There is the yearning. The feeling that I should be playing/writing. The feeling that I should be among others playing/writing. When I was a child it was easy to be among other players—my hometown, Mallow, had GAA and soccer clubs. Many of my friends played soccer and hurling and I could play with them on the street or in a local pitch. When I wanted to become a writer, I signed up for an MA in Creative Writing in University College Cork. I felt I needed tuition in writing (in the same way that I needed a coach when I was playing) and I needed to be among writers, in a community of writers. The instinct for both was correct, I felt comfortable being taught about craft and learning craft from my peers.

There is the communion. I felt at home among my writer classmates in UCC, just as I felt at home among my teammates when I played sport. But there is also the sense of friendship, shared purpose, and all that comes with them.

Then there is the honing of skills. As a child and a young man I practiced hurling and soccer and I was happy to practice, to develop the necessary skills, to get fit and to be a useful part of the team. I felt I belonged at those training sessions, the sense of purpose and moving toward a goal. When I became a writer I practiced my writing—day in and day out—redrafting, reworking, relearning. And I was happy to practice, I felt I belonged at my desk, with a sense of purpose and moving toward a goal.

In *On Boxing*, Joyce Carol Oates says that in sport the public sees only the final stage in a protracted, arduous, grueling and frequently despairing period of preparation. This is also true of art. The sweet and sharp poem that makes its way into the book was a lifetime in the making and stands tall on the hundreds of rejected poems and the thousands of hours of writing. The essence of sport and art is in that unseen protracted, arduous, gruelling and frequently despairing period of preparation. Very often, for the artist, this preparation is done alone. Likewise for the athlete, in the gym or pounding out the miles, alone on the road.

Then there is the doing. The day-to-day going to the desk, going to the studio, going to the track, going to the pitch, going to the gym. The acting out of the craft of the art and the self-exposition that must come with it. The failure or success, the getting up and getting on with it. The turning up, time after time.

This is art, this is sport.

* * *

I never knew as a child or as a young man that playing sport was a means of self-expression, a declaration of who I was and what I wanted and where I belonged. But I knew this in my writing immediately. I knew that in every story, every book, every piece of writing, I was putting myself down there on the page. I'm doing it right this moment and I will always do it—whether I am recognizable in the story or not. It is me, even if I am pretending to be somebody else in my fiction. This is art.

* * *

Fay Zwicky, the Australian poet, draws further similarities between art and sport. Sport and poetry, she says, require a balance between freedom of expression and restraint, between movement and constraint. A good poem and a good game can be described as graceful, playful and beautiful. Both involve movement (rhythm, propulsion, forward momentum) and flow. In "Border Crossings," Zwicky writes about the poet needing muscles, "emotional, spiritual and psychic muscles that transcend the limits of the self."

How often do we hear of an athlete being "poetry in motion"?

In an interview with Zwicky (not long before she died in 2017), the writer and sportswoman Charlotte Guest also speaks of the inherent beauty in sport. And this is where we often hear of the "art" of an Osaka or a Messi, in the sense of the aesthetic, the beauty or grace in their movement. Guest asks the question: "Are sport and poetry beautiful?" and she says that as abstract concepts, they are. But their main beauty is not so much as objects in their own right but "rather they possess a beauty that always reaches beyond itself, to something more … an ideal that is beautiful in its perfection."

Guest describes how the artist and the sportsperson are always striving for what they cannot make perfect, but how in that sense of infinity, creating art and playing sport make us forget our mortality.

* * *

In his poem "Sport," Paul Durcan is also comparing sport to art.

> It was my knowing
> That you were standing on the sideline
> That gave me the necessary motivation -
> That will to die
> That is as essential to sportsmen as to artists.

Durcan is conflating the intensity of sport and art, the compulsion of sport and art and the essential requirements of rigor and utter dedication (the willingness to die in order to succeed) in both sport and art.

The poem is also very much about the sharing of sport, in this case the sharing of a son with his father and the affirmation the son achieved from that.

* * *

Sport as an art form and its physical links to dance were reinforced for me when I went to see *Loch na hEala* in September 2019 in the Cork Opera House. The show is a fusion of dance, text and music—weaving a hybrid Martin McDonagh/Enda Walsh north Longford narrative via *Swan Lake and The Children of Lir*, with Nordic music. The protagonist, Jimmy, an unemployed and depressed man, is killed at the end of the story, as would be expected, but then there is what Judith Mackrell in *The Guardian* beautifully described as a rising to "an apotheosis of pure, visceral joy. Past yields to present and darkness gives way to light, as a snowstorm of feathers covers the stage and all 10 dancers and musicians unite in a larky Latin groove, which builds to a moment of rapture as unexpected as it is cathartic."

The silence of the dancers brought me back to scenes of sport. One, when I hurled as a boy, in snow. The other from *End Zone* by Don DeLillo when young American footballers play a game in falling snow.

> *It started to snow now, lightly at first, then more heavily, and in time it was almost impossible to see beyond the limits of the parade grounds. It was lovely to be hemmed in that way, everything white except for the clothes we wore and the football and the bundle of coats and books in the snow nearby … We were adrift within this time and place and what I experienced then, speaking just for myself, was some variety of environmental bliss.*

That's what I felt that night in the Cork Opera House, and what I feel when I am in the presence of a Caravaggio, and when I stand by The Pietà in St. Peter's Basilica in Rome, and at the chord shift a minute into "I Am All That I Need" by Fleet Foxes, and when listening to the audiobook of *Anything is Possible* by Elizabeth Strout or *Barbarian Days* by William Finnegan: adrift in time and space, within some variety of bliss.

* * *

There is a great risk-taking in sport. Players are vulnerable. There is every chance in sport that one will lose, but also that one will fail. I knew this in sport and now I know it in writing. Creating art and playing sport take bravery—not a physical bravery (although some sports do require this), but a bravery of the soul. When I send out a pitch to an agent, magazine, newspaper or publisher, there is every chance that it will be rejected—that I will fail and lose. I usually do. Hope and persistence are necessary in sport and writing. If the despair one feels from rejection is greater than the yearning to be read, to be acknowledged as a writer, then one stops writing. I have friends who did this. They were writers and now they are not. I know friends who gave up sport for the same reason. I gave up playing sport myself. Sport and art are callings, but they are also life choices—one can opt out more easily than one opts in.

You can argue that these failures and this yearning occupy other activities, too, even in our everyday lives, such as our work. But in sport and in art, there is the public exposure, the inviting in the reader or fan to judge the performance. This element, the willingness to risk public humiliation, is different from failing at a job or within a relationship.

* * *

I have been a reader for many years and I equate that to being a fan at a game. As a reader, I can pass judgment on the writing. I can reject it. When my first book was published in August 2018, I wrote a blog describing the terror of my exposure. It was like being a fan at a match, comfortable; and then climbing over the fence, putting on the team shirt and entering the game. Now I had to perform and all those in the crowd—the hurlers on the ditch—were looking at me, judging me, accepting or rejecting me.

Empathy is at the heart of reading and being a sports fan. As a fan, I am becoming the players on the pitch. I am living vicariously, through them. And, when one watches a Federer, this is a beautiful feeling. It is enriching. As a reader, I am also becoming the characters in the book. Through empathy, especially if the writer is very skillful, I feel the character's feelings. When I read *Conversations With Friends*, by Sally Rooney, I become Frances. I am a vulnerable young woman with an alcoholic father falling in love with a married man, and getting lost in that love.

And I want these feelings. I crave them because it means I'm alive. Even if Frances has her heart broken or does something vile, I want this to happen to me. This is why I read in the first place.

Children understand these links more than adults. Or perhaps they are just more open about it. When you sit down to watch a game with a child, they will ask: Who are you up for in this game? What they want to know is how you will perceive the game. Will you be one set of players or the other set of players? The adult might think she is watching objectively or without any real connection. The child will know that there's no such thing as objectivity in play. You are playing or not. And if you are playing, you want to win.

In her essay "Ok Son?" Wendy Erskine tells how when she would go to a film with her son (as a child) he would ask at the beginning of the film: Which person are you in this? He knew that, in order to engage in the story, we have to be one of the characters. Of course we do. In fact, we can be all the characters if it's done well. But there is no point in any story if we're not right in it.

And, of course, who we are in the story determines how the story will turn out for us.

It's the same in sport. A game is a story. When the child asks you who you are up for at the beginning of the game, in fact she is asking who you are in the game. We're not spectators, we're in the game, we're right in there.

* * *

In her book *Wanderlust*, Rebecca Solnit describes her feelings when she came on to the streets with thousands of others to demonstrate against the 1991 U.S. Gulf War. In those moments of shared belief and the shared expression of that belief, she says, she sensed a rare and magical possibility of a populist communion.

In those moments, she senses that the "small pool" of her own identity has been overrun by a great flood, "bringing its own grand collective desires and resentments, scouring out that pool so thoroughly that one no longer feels fear or sees the reflections of one's self."

She says that these people, in the right circumstances of idealism or outrage, become heroes. Heroes, she describes as people so motivated by ideals that fear cannot sway them. And in the moments of shared action for what is good, everyone present becomes a hero.

Those who attend games and take part in games as fans are not heroes. But those inside the white lines have been motivated so strongly that fear cannot sway them. And so, they put themselves on display to be judged and to risk failure in public and shaming circumstances. They have dedicated their lives to become the hero and, as fans, because we are present within and participating in that moment, we are becoming the hero too. Our fear cannot sway us during the game, our failures have no purchase on us, our mistakes are erased in the greatness and glory unfolding during the game.

And that feeling is truly wonderful.

* * *

James S. Vass Jr. says that when fans go to a game, they do it to experience the phenomenon of "cheering for self."

There are two transformations at the game (and he writes in the context of a college basketball game)—although he refers to the game as "an event," which includes all that happens before, during and after the game. This is a distinction I strongly agree with. So much of sport happens before and after the game—especially its rituals.

The first transformation is that the person going to the event steps into the role of fan. Before the event, the fan might be a housewife, physician, student, judge, policeman—anything. But when they attend the game they are transformed into the fan and only the fan. They become homogeneous. This process is similar to when we pick up a book. Before we pick up the novel *Brooklyn* by Colm Tóibín we may be a criminal or a saint, but while we are reading the book, we are all readers.

The second transformation is that the fan becomes the player—the star. "Players," writes Vass, "become a proxy for those that no longer play basketball, cannot or never could. Players become representations for fans that identify with the team of players and who share the credit for success and the agony of defeat." This transformation then allows them (and this is what fans most want) to "bask in the glory of the chosen team's success."

This second transformation also takes place when we are reading *Brooklyn*. As readers, we become Eilis—we feel her feelings, we are joyful at her joy, we are fearful at her fears, we are loving at her love. We bask in her life while we are reading. When she is successful, happy or sad, so are we. And we want this. It's why we picked up the book or watched the movie in the first place, why we engage with all types of art.

* * *

Art is about emotion. The whole purpose of music, writing, painting, film-making—all of it—is emotion. It's about feeling something. Henry James said that in the arts "feeling is meaning."

Art is not an intellectual exercise, even if one has to use the brain to write the poem or the symphony and one has to use the brain to process them. Once we translate that, it is all distilled down to an intense emotion. We want to be Romeo and Juliet. We want to die for love. We want, like Mephisto, to sell our souls to the devil.

It's the same in sport. We engage with our team or the player we love (an emotion) because we want to feel what they feel. We want to feel young and fit and beautiful and purposeful. We want to have the skill they have and to know we have that skill. It doesn't matter whether we win or lose (and we want to win for sure, but the risk is worth the emotional investment) as much as whether we feel or we don't. Winning is the best thing, but losing is the second best thing.

And these feelings are in the body. They are not intellectual, they are physical. We feel with our bodies. With our skin, our eyes, our hair, our heart, our lungs, our mouth. Our mouth goes dry in awe of Van Gogh and in awe of Simone Biles. Our heart beats faster, our skin tightens, our hair stands up, our breath quickens. While sport in its enaction is physical, our responses are physical too.

* * *

When I do a reading at an event I expose myself publicly. I know I could make a mess of it. I know the audience might hate my work, or feel indifferent to it. I feel sick with nerves beforehand. I ask myself why do I put myself through this. If the event were cancelled I'd be delighted. If nobody turned up, I'd be delighted. These are the exact same feelings I had before a match. The madness of it all, the sheer arrogance to think that I could play well, that I could win. And then—afterwards—the relief. The utter joy that it's over. The pride, the basking in public recognition, the sense of being accepted, and worthy and valuable.

This is sport.
This is art.

* * *

In her book *Living, Thinking, Looking* the American writer Siri Hustvedt writes about the similarities between playing and writing. One of the most damning accusations of sport is that it is useless. People like Chomsky and Eco, Perelman and Brohm look on sport as a distraction from the important aspects of life. But, as Hustvedt points out: was the work of Emily Dickinson useful? Was the writing of Kafka useful? Both of them, for the most part, did not send out their work and Kafka directed that his be destroyed when he died. Art, ultimately, Hustvedt says, is useless. You cannot sit on a painting, you cannot eat a sculpture or use music as a tool. The only purpose for art is to be looked at, thought about and felt. This is true of sport, too. A game will not feed us or clothe us or shelter us. But, like art, it is alive and we want to look at it and think about it and feel it and be transformed by it.

Those who deride sport as a meaningless, physical and often brutal activity (Orwell) would never point to the meaninglessness of Beethoven's *Fifth Symphony*. Because they are moved by music it is meaningful and because they are not moved by sport is it meaningless. They can see the truth in music and therefore it has significance. But I can see the truth in sport and so it is significant for me.

Hustvedt champions the views of D.W. Winnicott, the English pediatrician and psychoanalyst. Winnicott followed on from Freud's *Tummelplatz* and Strachey's playground theories to talk about "potential or transitional space." He theorized that it was only through play that people could feel real. And I see this in sport all the time. One of the reasons people are so addicted to sport and why it is so popular is that it feels more real than real life—what Joyce Carol Oates calls *ordinary life*. The boxer, she says, prefers physical pain in the ring to the absence of pain that is ideally the condition of ordinary life.

In sport we feel that we are in a kind of hyper-reality. This intermediate area, according to Winnicott, is crowded with illusions generated by play, but the "potential space" cannot be situated only inside the person. It is outside the individual but it is also not the external "real" world. The transitional object, he says (in the case of a child this could be a teddy bear or a blanket) is a real object in the world, but also a symbol—it is at once a "piece of real experience" and a fiction.

The origins of play are deep and bodily, according to Winnicott. They begin in the first relationship between the child and the mother, in the mirroring that happens there. Play (sport) is the physical exploration of space and our ability to create an imaginary zone of experience: potential space. Hustvedt says that this is where art lives, but for me it is also where sport lives, where our appreciation of sport becomes rooted inside us and whence our love of sport grows.

While the embedding of play is in early infancy, the embedding of sport is in childhood. So, too, is our art embedded in childhood. Louise Bourgeois said that art is not about art. Art is about life. "All my work … all my subjects have found their inspiration in my childhood," a childhood that never lost its mystery or drama. The wonder of George Best's perfection (which I experienced in my childhood) has never lost its mystery and drama for me.

* * *

Games are a fiction—they are not real. Sport is often described as a metaphor (by Simon Barnes among others) or an allegory (by Donal Ryan among others). Games are just games, just playing. They are not real (in the sense that they are meaningless)—and yet they are very real because we imbue them with meaning. This is true of all the arts. A painting is meaningless—it is just some bits of colored material spread around a canvas. But, when this is done by Caravaggio it is art—it means everything. A game of soccer is just twenty-two men or women chasing a bag of air around a field—meaningless. But when your team wins the League of Ireland or the World Cup, it means everything.

It is the truth in Caravaggio that makes it real and engaging. It is the truth in sport that also makes it real and engaging. This engagement, to paraphrase Hustvedt, is "active and creative" not just intellectually, but "emotionally, physically, consciously and unconsciously."

Some see this truth in art, some see it in music, some see it in poetry or drama, and I am lucky enough to be one of those people who see the truth in all of those. I don't think it's mainly snobbery that causes some intellectuals to look down on sport (compared to art); some people just don't see the truth there.

I, along with billions of others, do.

* * *

Music, painting, dance, and literature (all the arts) Hustvedt says, are generated by play. But sport, too, is generated by play. We play sport. Winnicott says we never give up our fictions for the so-called real world. The direct development he traces from transitional phenomena to playing, to shared playing to cultural experiences is the exact sporting path I took as a child. I played alone with my football around my house. My ball was my transitional object. But as I grew older, playing alone wasn't enough: I wanted shared playing and cultural experiences.

It's not just Hustvedt and Winnicott. Johan Huizinga, the Dutch cultural historian, argued that all culture is a form of play. Lev Vygotsky, the Soviet Marxist psychologist, felt that play, a developmental phenomenon, began with the imaginary situation. When a child pretends, she "operates with alienated meaning in a real situation"—the symbol has shifted. When we play and when we play sport, we are operating in a real situation (a game) but the meaning is alienated. In real life, the painting is just blobs of paint on a canvas, the book is ink markings on pages, soccer is twenty-two players chasing a bag of air around a field. But in play—in imagination—there is a monster under the bed, a fairy flying outside the window, and the result of the game we are playing has a significance beyond understanding and will transform our lives and render us so joyful that we can barely continue to breathe.

As I am kicking my ball around my childhood home, I am also happily lost in Vygotsky's imaginary situation. When I chip the ball into my dog's kennel, I am George Best passing it to Denis Law who buries it. When I bend it around the corner of the house, I am Rivelino bending the ball around the German wall. I am in the most real of situations in my childhood home, but the meaning of my game is alienated, thanks to my imagination, which is fired with magic.

* * *

A similar process also takes place within the fans, who participate in the play differently from players, but participate nonetheless. In 1996 scientists discovered that neurons in the premotor cortex of macaque monkeys' brains fired when they performed an action such as grasping. But these neurons also fire when another animal merely observes the same action. These are called mirror neurons. In sport, fans can develop a type of human intersubjectivity. We know we are not the players on the field carrying out acts of wonder and glory, but our mirror neurons still fire, allowing us to feel as the players do. Hustvedt refers to this as a type of biological *mimesis*. Plato knew of this *mimesis* and applied it to the arts, but it was not proven as a biological fact for another 2,000 years in the macaque monkey.

It's as if the game throws up a mirror through which we are permitted to see a greater version of ourselves. It only happens when the game is on, which renders this time magical. When the game is over, we are transformed back to ourselves, with our losses and failures and worries and beer bellies intact. The same thing happens when we see a masterpiece of film, say, *Wild Strawberries* by Ingmar Bergman. The film throws up a mirror whereby we see ourselves as an egotistical professor who is forced to re-evaluate his life. During the film we are that professor. The film transforms us. But when the film ends and we leave the cinema, our own existence creeps back in. This is art. This is sport.

In a way, there is a dialogue between us and the players in the game and we recognize ourselves in the players, as the baby recognizes herself in her mother. This reflection—of a better version of ourselves—is something fans of sport utterly desire and we believe it to be true.

Babies are not born with a sense of self, they do not learn it until they are about two when they develop the ability to reflect on themselves from the perspective of others. In a way, when we engage with art or sport, we deliberately "unlearn" this skill and give up our own sense of selves to experience the thrill of having the sense of being somebody else.

When trying to teach young students how writing and reading works, I use a plot device of J.K. Rowling in the Harry Potter series of books. It is called *Polyjuice Potion* and when a character takes it they assume the form of another person. But they have to have something from the body of the other person (a hair, for example) to make the potion work. In writing, the magic is more powerful, I argue, because one doesn't just assume the form of another, one becomes the other. Because the writer has used something so specific to the character (her essence), we can cross over into the book, or the scene in the book, and become that person. So, at the end of *Foster* by Claire Keegan, the writing is so perfect that we become the nameless child as she runs to embrace the aunt and uncle who have shown her a love she had never known before. As she runs down the road toward the gate where they are stopped, the reader is utterly transformed into that child. We run, too.

This transformation takes place during games. When I watched Séamus Callanan score a goal in an All-Ireland hurling semi-final in 2019, I was so inside the game and the moment and the hurling, that for a second I became that great hurler—it was just for a moment, but I was completely him. I had to steady myself by holding on to the bar counter, so enraptured I had become at scoring such a goal in such a game. The transformation into Séamus was so vivid as to be truly jarring and so was the transformation back into myself afterwards in the sunshine outside the bar. The person who takes *Polyjuice Potion* feels strange when returning to themselves. I feel strange when I return to myself having been in a great book or a great film or a great game.

* * *

In *On Boxing* Joyce Carol Oates compares watching the great fights between Joe Louis and Billy Conn, Joe Frazier and Muhammad Ali, Marvin Hagler and Thomas Hearns to enjoying a perfectly executed rendition of Bach's *Well-Tempered Clavier*. The story's mystery, she says, is that so much happens so swiftly and with such heart-stopping subtlety that you cannot absorb it except to know that "something profound is happening and it is happening in a place beyond words."

But, just because a match is a story without words, it doesn't mean that it has no text or no language, or that it is "brute," "primitive" or "inarticulate." Rather, the text is improvised in action, Oates says; and the language between the fighters is a dialogue "of the most refined sort" in a joint response to "the mysterious will of the audience which is always that the fight be a worthy one." Only by being worthy can the match overcome the crude paraphernalia of the setting (ring, lights, ropes, stained canvas, sweat, blood, etc.) with its transcendent action. Only by being worthy will the artifice fully work.

The difficulty for the non-initiated into sport is that they cannot see beyond the setting or hear beyond what they judge as the brute inarticulacy of the action that is taking place. For them it is like reading dialogue in a language they don't know. I have friends I meet at matches who would never dream of reading a novel, or listening to music. They would say to me: "I'm not into reading or music." The language of music to them is inarticulate. They don't see the truth in fiction.

For me, the lack of words in sport is not a drawback. There are many types of language and communication and there are no words in much of the music of Max Richter, Ennio Morricone or Miles Davis. But it does occur to me that in writing about sport in fiction or in non-fiction that I am a translator of sorts. What I'm articulating is not my own, I'm taking the art and trying to find the right words to describe it.

I'm okay with that. It's an honorable role and if I can do it correctly, I will bring the unwritten profundity of sport back from a place beyond words, to a place where we all can hear its story. My astonishment is your astonishment—to paraphrase Annie Dillard.

* * *

Another difficulty for some people is the lack of a script in sport. The absence of the master creative artist who has written something wonderful. Oates says that while a match is a story, it is always a wayward story, one in which anything can happen. There is no libretto, no text. In sport the text is writing itself as it goes and it may be a grand drama or not. To the sportsperson, this is actually one of the great attractions of sport. Nobody knows what will happen.

Dermot Bolger, who wrote two plays about identity that hinged around fans of the Irish soccer team (*High Germany,* 1990, and *The Parting Glass,* 2010), says that one of the things fans love so much about sport is that it is not a previously devised text. In effect, the players and the fans are composing the work as they go along. Nobody knows the ending—it has not been written yet. It is, as Oates says, being improvised in action.

This is a thrilling idea. That all the 82,000 people present at the All-Ireland Hurling Final and the million people watching on TV are creating the story of the game as it happens—the ultimate performative act. Of course the players are the main playwrights, but everybody has a role. Second by second, the tension and drama build to the ending that nobody knows. We watch, not knowing but also loving the not knowing. The players, Oates says, are like shadow-selves of each other, but they are also shadow-selves of everyone watching—the million or more people in the game. Aristotle defined tragedy as something "serious, complete and of a certain magnitude" and this is what we want of sport, too.

It matters who wins, of course it does. But what matters more is that the game is worthy and when that happens, it's more than enough for us. My books may never win prizes or become bestsellers, but if somebody reads them and tells me they were moved, then my books are worthy and that's more than enough for me. In any case, I gave them my best shot.

That is more than enough in sport and more than enough in art.

Poet, Poet, You Stand Alone

I had one unit of poetry in a college English class with a professor named Roger who had long hair even though he was old and smoked a pipe and played the banjo and had studied with OWEN BARFIELD!!! I wrote perhaps the stupidest poem in history for Roger, called "Goalie," about a goalie, that repeated the line "Goalie, Goalie, you stand alone," throughout. And even though I'd never really been into hockey or soccer or lacrosse or any other sport requiring a goalie, like water polo, in which case the line would have had to be "Goalie, Goalie, you tread water alone," Roger gave me the coveted + grade because I completed the assignment and hey, man, poetry isn't about grades, and scribbled something like, "Try to think about more things than sports" on my paper. I returned to my dorm room that afternoon deep in thought, but not reassessing my relationship to sports—after all I was in school with Magic Johnson and Kirk Gibson, neither of whose jock Owen Barfield could carry—but feeling generally disappointed that Roger had not fully recognized my genius and recommended my poem and its haunting repetitive paean to athletic loneliness for the university's literary magazine.

Jeffrey Munroe

Take Your Mark:
Excerpts from a Novel-in-Progress

Anne Greenawalt

Summary: When members of an elite age group swimming girls' medley relay team reconvene as adults at a fundraiser for their club team, their old coach challenges them to train for and compete in a master's swim meet, an international swimming league for adults 18 years and older. Each woman has a different relationship with herself, her body, and her swimming history, and this challenge reopens childhood wounds that never fully healed. Their return to swimming forces the women to revisit and reflect on the highs and lows of their elite childhood swimming careers. Through scrapbook items like photos, newspaper articles, notes passed in class, training logs, journal entries, art projects, interviews, and other bricolage in addition to traditional narrative, this story follows the girls through age group national victories, to top-tier boarding schools, to college where only two of them were still competing, and into adulthood where they thought they had moved on with their lives but are still products of their early swimming careers. This novel is an exploration of the adult lives of former swimmers and how that early sports career shaped the rest of their lives in ways they could have never anticipated. This excerpt shares fragments of the women's stories as they contemplate whether to accept their coach's challenge.

Olivia (Backstroker)

When I heard the idea, I laughed. I'm still not sure if it was joyful or maniacal. Me, swimming again? I hung up my racing suit in high school. Early high school. Haven't swum laps since. Took up smoking and drinking instead. And art. No, I haven't gotten particularly fat—I've been blessed with a good metabolism. My lifestyle isn't very conducive to exercise. I mean, I walk the dogs, several times a day, if that counts for anything.

I'm happy. I've got the life I want. I wake up whenever I want to or whenever the dogs are persuasive enough. Spend most days in my studio, which is most of my apartment except for the small corner where I eat and the other corner where I sleep. In the evenings, I go to a show or a gallery or just to a bar to socialize, network, that sort of thing. I've been learning to do a lot of that digitally, social media, and all that, but nice to have some in-person social interactions, too, you know? Then I go to bed whenever I want. It's great.

I mean, I'm not making big bucks or anything. I'm not famous. I live and work in a studio apartment. But it's enough. I'm happy, as I said. Many artists do that broody thing because it fuels them. Not me. And it's not like my life and the world are all rainbows and butterflies. But maybe my outlook on it is? Well, now it is.

Yeah, most of my work has some kind of water theme. That's kind of my signature style. I guess you'd be surprised to know, then, that I don't miss swimming, rarely even think about the competitive swimming world anymore, except when someone asks about it. Yeah, it shaped my younger self, clearly had an influence. You ask most former age-group swimmers, especially those who competed at a national or higher level, and they'll tell you, "Once a swimmer, always a swimmer."

I don't feel like a swimmer. Not anymore. Don't identify as one. Now? I'm an artist. And a dog mom. And I'm OK with that. I'm someone who used to swim.

Yeah, I guess that's true: I didn't just swim when I was younger; I was a swimmer. They tell me a really good one, too. And that's cool. I look back with fond memories, but almost like I'm looking back at someone else, someone else's life and accomplishments, you know?

I couldn't just jump in the pool now and be fast. Maybe faster than people who have never swum before, sure. But what you're asking will require time. Training. Effort. I just don't know that I have it in me anymore.

Ally (Breaststroker)

I don't want to swim again. That was my first thought. Why would I? I wasted my entire childhood and young adulthood chasing a dream I could never catch, spent years brutalizing my body with nine plus swimming workouts per week, totaling about 72,000 yards per week—that's, like, over 40 miles!—plus strength and conditioning sessions three to four times per week. I hurt. All. The. Time. I found this old notebook—a training log that my college coach suggested I keep—that documented my workouts, my food, and how I felt. Nothing fancy, just a $.99 composition book. It's completely filled with a full season's worth of notes.

In the "how I felt" sections every day I wrote either tired, angry, or tired and angry.

And that was my life. Every day. For 23 years. Minus a few years of my infancy, but even then, I was in parent/child swim classes before I was a year old.

So, yeah, my first thought was no, I don't want to swim again.

* * *

I've heard enough stories, met enough athletes to know that's just part of being an athlete, the tiredness and single-minded dedication. Go through the pain, do what you've got to do to get to where you want to be. I don't think there's a single person who would say I didn't work hard enough, train right, eat right, or concentrate hard enough.

I'm sick to my stomach thinking of all the things I put on hold or gave up for swimming. And for what? Third place. Third place by three one hundredths of a second. Another by two tenths of a second. If second place is like kissing your brother, what does that make third place like? Like kissing the underside of an unwashed toilet seat. A public one. At a gas station.

It wasn't, like, a bronze medal at the Olympics kind of third place. Even the worst losers in the world would have to smile for an Olympics bronze. It was an I-don't-even-qualify-for-the-Olympics third place because only the top two in each event go. There are some exceptions to that, but not in my events. 200 breast, 100 breast. .03 seconds. .2 seconds. French kissing a toilet seat.

So, yeah, that 100 breast was my last event, last race, last time swimming laps. Ever. Twenty years ago.

So, no, I'm not eager to put on a practice suit and swim up and down the pool, chasing the black line for hours and hours and...

No, thank you. I'll gracefully bow out of this one.

* * *

My coach at the time, my college coach, tried to get me to do a shake-out swim with the team the next day, but I said nope. I wouldn't do it. Didn't want all of the pitying looks, the I'm so sorries, the you'll-get-it-next-times. There would be no next time. I was already twenty-three years old, already a grandma by swimming standards, already graduated from college—barely graduated from college—so it wasn't like I was dependent on swimming for scholarships anymore. Done and done.

Did you hear that the local TV station wanted to send a TV crew to my home—my home—to film my reaction watching the 200 breast finals during the Olympics? What the fuck is wrong with people? Capitalizing on my loss? That was a no. A big no. I haven't trusted journalists since. I've known you, though, since we were kids. Maybe you're different. Maybe I can trust you. Maybe not.

* * *

July, she was there, at the trials. I know from the email she sent me later that week that she spoke to me in the locker room after the 100 breast. I don't remember that. I didn't want to speak to anyone after those races, but if there was one person in the world I would have been willing to talk to, it would have been her. But I don't remember. It's like what I read about in psych class: how people suppress traumatic memories. Self-preservation, that sort of thing.

I do remember the email. Still have the email, somewhere, but haven't read it in twenty years or so. No, I never responded. We're friends on Facebook, but haven't seen or spoken with her since then. I'm not angry with her. Why would I be angry at her? But, really, what is there left to say?

July (Butterflier)

I'm all for it! It's not like I ever really wanted to stop swimming, but I did because, you know, life? I'd swim here and there when I could. Even now I swim, I dunno, a couple times a month. I take my kids. They swim, were on a team but then their lives took them in different directions, too. Jordan runs cross country. Jesse plays, like five different instruments. Little Janna Banana asked to do martial arts when she was three. Three! She's taken judo, karate, Tae Kwon Do, and then went back to judo. Wants to be the next Ronda Rousey and fight in the MMA circuit. I told her to go for it. I told her swimming is good cross-training, so she'll still swim on the summer league. Might swim in high school, too. We'll see.

I have my practice, too, as a health and wellness coach. Or a life coach. Same thing to me. And I'm not associated with one of those pyramid schemes. I have my degrees in nutrition and exercise science and a master's in counseling. That took all of my time and attention to get established—which I did while conceiving, carrying, birthing, and parenting three children and being attentive to their needs and goals.

Well, yeah, my husband is amazing. That goes without saying. He has been super supportive of my career goals. He had a steady job … but what he really wanted was a big family, so, yeah, I'd say we're supportive of each other's goals. He's a stay-at-home dad. Which is really amazing. We're both getting to do what we love. It was perfect timing. Janna was born right around the time my practice was taking off. We're all just really in synch. Now I'm established and thriving at my practice. My youngest is eleven years old. So, now maybe I have a shift about to happen. It might open some space for me to work on my goals apart from career and family, my own health and wellness goals. For me, this proposal is good timing.

As a competitive swimmer, I accomplished more than I ever thought possible, from national age group records starting at ten & under to wins at NCAA championships, Olympic trials qualifying times, and making semi-finals at trials in two events. Yes, I am super proud of that. Some people think that unless you have an Olympic medal, it means nothing. I never thought I'd win nationals in college. I never thought I'd make a Trials cut. Swimming at semi-finals was like a fairy tale. Sometimes I still don't believe it was me who did that. Those were never my goals—they just happened.

If they had been goals? I have some theories about that. If those were my goals, I would have probably gotten too nervous, psyched myself out. I did that a lot as a kid, so I stopped setting lofty, fantasy goals. On the other hand, there's some pretty compelling research that argues that maybe I could have finaled at trials, maybe even made the Olympics if I had set my sights on it, dreamed bigger, believed I could. I don't know. I don't want to talk about that. I don't think it's helpful to dwell on what could have been. I was a good swimmer, a very good one, and I'm happy with how my career ended.

Maisie (Freestyler)

I like the idea but I'm the only one of the four of us who has been swimming, and I don't sprint or swim in pools anymore. So, I think it'll be a tough sell. If it were just up to me? Open water relay! I think that would be even more difficult to convince them to do. I'm OK with this, I think. I'm just not sure about doing flip turns, you know, because of my back.

I've done some open water races. A few 5K and 10K lake swims. An eight-mile river swim, with the current. Did the swimming leg of some local triathlons with friends. Haven't done any swimming in the ocean because what if a wave caught me? Sent me tumbling? Not sure how my back would react to that. Not well.

My back … I guess it doesn't really stop me from doing much anymore. I'm not as wild as I used to be. I'm a risk assessment analyst for an insurance company, so I live vicariously through our customers now. My husband and I have two children, two boys, who have a lot of me in them. That former rough and tumble me. They play all of the physical sports—football, hockey, rugby—and all of the other ones, too. They keep us busy. We told them they'd need to narrow down their sports list when they get to high school. There's this award for graduating seniors who play three varsity sports all four years. They want that award. I don't even know how they know about it. Yeah, they swim. They're good swimmers, but that's not where their hearts are, and that's cool.

That rough and tumble lifestyle—I don't have time to miss it because I live it through my kids every day. After the accident, I just didn't want it anymore, didn't let myself want it. At first, I guess I missed it. Total lifestyle changer, for sure. But I'm not that person anymore. I sometimes wonder what my husband and children—or any of my college or adult friends—would think of me if they had known me then. I think it would shock them. Sure, I've got my open water swimming and I'll often swim alone, which has its risks, but beyond that? I haven't rollerbladed, ice skated, ridden rollercoasters, played any other sports since then. I never had the chance to go skydiving or hang gliding. Bungee jumping was a big thing when I was a kid, but I never got to do it. No, I definitely haven't gone rock climbing again. No, you already asked me that—I don't miss pool swimming. But I will tell you, I love seeing that spirit in my boys. I love that they'll try anything. They have some caution but no fear. I've tried very hard, very deliberately not to let my limited lifestyle affect them. I encourage them to take risks. I do. Like when we were at the lake swing, I talked to them about what to look for: was the water deep enough? Any areas of wear on the rope attached to the tree? Anything in the water they could hit? Could anything above them fall on them? They're really good about it. The youngest said he'd make sure to let his big brother test it out first! They're getting it, though. Taking risks, calculated ones.

Olivia (Backstroker)

"I don't want to swim." This is Ollie's mantra as she stares out the window while hovering over the kitchen sink eating a half an English muffin smeared with almond butter. Crumbs snow into the sink, mirroring the actual snow that falls outside, and creates little ski slopes on the outer windowsill.

Ollie wears a hooded sweatshirt, slippers, and boxer shorts that exposed knees still tanned from a summer of walking her dogs through every state park in Pennsylvania. She couldn't remember when she had last shaved. If she went swimming, a little hair on her knees was the least of her problems. To go swimming, she'd have to change, or at least put on pants. Then she'd have to strip down again in the locker room at the gym, which had those massive fans running all year long, which was nice when coming in from a hike in the ninety-degree humidity, but not from the pool which was already like swimming in an arctic stream. She imagined walking—shivering—from the locker room onto the pool deck. She never understood how all of the swim team parents, all swimming spectators ever of all time, complained about the hot, humid pool decks. She was always the swimmer with the parka pulled tight around her, hood up over a woolen winter hat, sweatpants, and knee-high socks. Other swimmers loved her socks. She'd get new pairs every year for Christmas, birthdays. Her favorites were the hot pink ones with the little fuzzy snow bunnies that Maisie had given her after she broke a minute in the 100 backstroke for the first time when she was fifteen. She didn't get cold like that anywhere other than a pool deck.

Once she got through the locker room, she'd sit on the pool's edge and watch the glazed-water surface if untouched by other swimmers, choppy if others had beaten her to it. She'd watch and build up the nerve to sink herself into that water, one inch at a time, starting with a big toe. She'd brace her arms on the deck, lower herself in. Ally used this method, too, she remembered, but not July or Maisie who just jumped in, were always the firsts to jump in, splashing the rest of them on entry.

After she got in, she would swim for an hour or so, maybe ninety minutes if there were no twinges in her shoulders. Her body would eventually warm up, or at least it always used to. Maybe she'd even sweat. No one believes that swimmers sweat in the water. They do. It's just immediately whisked away by the clouds of chemical water where it mixes with other swimmers' sweat and their other bodily fluids. She wasn't squeamish, didn't think about the other body fluids in the water—or at least didn't think about them too much, even when she saw the pale-yellow clouds of ammonia drift up from the swim trunks of the eighty-year-old men who floated in the free swim area—but it did turn her stomach every time she saw a Band-Aid float up from the bottom of the pool. The worst, though, was when a thick, dark tumbleweed of someone else's hair weaved itself between her fingers and no amount of shaking would disturb it once it latched on. She'd have to stop and peel it off, strand-by-strand, fighting her gag reflex with each hair until her hand was free.

When she finishes the workout, she'll have to brave the cold of the locker room again, this time soaking wet. Just thinking about it gives her goosebumps, so if the little hairs on her tanned knees weren't already sticking out, they are now. She chews the last bit of English muffin and thinks about what it will feel like to exit the gym into the winter wonderland. Wet hair turning crunchy beneath a woolen winter hat.

The studio apartment, as always, is so silent she can hear the silence, except for the dogs' gentle snores. Even the dogs were smart enough to still be asleep. But then the text message chime of the phone she'd tucked into the pocket of the sweatshirt breaks the calm.

"Get your ass to the pool."

She smiled. Hundreds of miles apart, more than a decade since their last reunion, and Ally still knows her, still predicts Ollie's movements the way she had to hundreds of times before to predict the timing of Ollie's lunges into the wall and determine when to start the wind up of her relay start.

Ally (Breaststroker)

When she stretches her legs before getting out of bed the next morning, her calves tighten into hard little balls, borderline charley horse in each leg. But it is worse when she gets out of bed and limps to the bathroom where she can't sit down on the toilet because of the tightness and pain in her quads, hips, and glutes. She has to brace herself with her hands on either side of the toilet seat and slowly lower down using her arm strength and ignoring her legs. Once she is down, she thinks, fuck. Stuck. She finishes, wipes, then reaches out for the towel rack in front of the toilet and uses it like a chin up bar to stand up. Just as she pulls herself to a full stand, the bar cracks twice and disconnects from the wall, forcing her to stumble sideways and hit her hips on the sink. Fuck! She says it louder this time then pauses, listening through the silence to determine if she woke anyone else. She puts down the broken towel rack on the back of the toilet because she doesn't know where else to put it other than the floor, and there is no way in fuck she is going to bend over to put it on the floor.

Her first "adult" swim was last night, at eight p.m. because she had to wait for the swim team to finish. She had printed out an old workout from college, the shortest one she could find, and put it in a plastic bag so the paper wouldn't disintegrate at the end of the pool. 5,000 yards with a 1,000-yard warm up? Surely she could do that. Maybe she couldn't make all of the interval times, like 1:15's for repeat 100 IM's, but she could adjust the times as she went.

Fuck. She says it again, but this time just in her head as she looks in the mirror. Last night's goggle marks have almost dissolved from beneath her eyes, or were those just bruises from everyday tiredness? She doesn't recognize herself. Sure, there are her eyes, large brown almonds and her brownish hair, smashed down on one side from however she had slept that night. Her teeth are the same shape. Her lips … she had never really studied those, but no noticeable difference now. It is the rest of her body. It isn't hers anymore. It is soft and pale and sits in pudges around her hips and under her butt. And her lats are puffy and display none of their former definition. Her jawline is all but nonexistent. Her thighs, she realizes—and this is the worst part—have gotten this cottage cheese texture to them.

"Where did it go?" she asks out loud, but she knows it is still in there, can feel it trying to rip its way out.

Her over-confidence and stubbornness, as always, had gotten the best of her. She muscled her way through all 5,000 yards, even though her shoulders were grinding mid-way through. She felt like she had forgotten how to breathe, how to rotate, how to point her toes for the most efficient flutter kick. Even when she switched to breaststroke, her body didn't quite remember what to do, her hips screaming in protest. Ouch, stop that, they wailed, but she didn't listen. She figured they just needed to get warmed up and she pushed them through the pain kick after kick after kick.

The entire left side of her upper body flinches when she reaches for her toothbrush: the deltoid, pecs, and lats feeling like they have all expanded with Elephantitis and are grinding against each other. She rotates her head from side to side, then rolls it down and to the right, then the opposite way, feeling the tightness radiate from her trapezoids, up her neck, onto the base of her skull. She shoves a thumb in a groove that connects her head to her neck and holds the thumb there. A marble of knotted muscle fights back, fights back, fights back, and then relaxes and her thumb slips off of it.

Fuck, she thinks. This is going to be a long day.

July (Butterflier)

It yanked on her from the inside. That's the only way she could describe it. The tendon, or whatever soft tissues were in there, yanked on her bone—on her nerve endings—with each stroke. There was no pain. Yet. Just a little tug. An annoyance, like a little sister tugging on the hem of your skirt to get your attention. Not a big deal, but if you ignored her, she would pull harder and harder until she ripped it, and harder still until she tore the whole damn thing off of your waist, leaving you feeling angry, frustrated, and a little bit foolish for ignoring her.

A decade since she had last swum laps with any urgency, and that tug was still there in her left shoulder. It was OK, for now, for the thirty minutes or so she forced herself to be in the water. But she knew what would come when she revived her fitness, when she felt more confident, when she swam again as if her life depended on it.

Every day after high school practice, the high school coach—not Coach Owen—made her go to the training room where someone would make her scoop ice from the freezer with a metal shovel and put it in a plastic bag then wait in line for someone else to saran wrap it around her shoulder, under her armpit, across her chest. Sometimes she got ice bags for both shoulders, just to be safe, but usually it was just for the left one. Afterwards, she'd ride shotgun home in her dad's car, or sometimes in the backseat with Ollie in one of her brothers' cars, and the ice would melt and drip down her chest, between her breasts. It was worse in the winter, packing ice on her skin then stepping out into a snowstorm. The bags put enough bulk on her arms that her normal winter coat wouldn't fit over them. She just had to drape the coat over her shoulders and pray it wasn't a windy evening.

She didn't want the ice bags again, or the ultrasound treatments the trainers at the high school gave her when the pain got so bad that she couldn't lift her arms above her head to brush or shampoo her own hair. Yes, she was done with that.

But she had committed to this.

She was older, yeah, but a little wiser, too, she hoped. She never really worked her therapy bands, back then. Didn't like weight room strength training. But there are so many more options now than then, right? Yoga. Pilates. Boot Camp. TRX. She could strengthen that shoulder. Build up slowly. Be smart.

Maisie (Freestyler)

The door from the locker latched shut behind her and Maisie felt as if she'd been locked in a dungeon. The pool was in the basement of the high school, so there were no windows, and the only exits were the heavy steel locker room doors. A few long fluorescent lights lined the perimeter of the paneled ceiling but only illuminated the deck as well as a dim flashlight bulb in the belly of a forest.

The four-foot-deep pool had four lanes, two of which were designated as open swim lanes for children playing or others who just wanted to float or water walk. Just float, she repeated in her head and laughed to herself. Her first "exercise," months after the accident, was to float in the pool with one of those floatation belts that the old ladies used for water aerobics classes. "What if I can float without it?" Maisie had asked the physical therapist. She told

Maisie not to strain herself, and Maisie laughed out loud thinking about how a twenty-minute float session—with a floatation device—would compare to her usual two-and-a-half-hour daily swim practices that included dry land and at least 8,000 yards. "That's about five miles," she'd tell non-swimmers.

Of the two lap lanes, an aqua jogger occupied one of them, which left one lane for Maisie, the end lane. End lanes made Maisie's stomach turn because of the crust and oil and Band-Aids and hairballs that got stuck in the corners. She could already see the corners were brown with rust, or dirt. She had a sudden desire for socks, for her feet to be covered, protected. But nobody swims with socks.

Maisie picked up a kickboard from the bin against the wall and then put it on the deck behind the lane. She sat on it, unwilling to let even a portion of her skin make contact with the pool deck that had that same dirty rust color between each tile.

While sitting, legs dangling over the edge, feet covered in pool water—not too cold, she noted—up to her ankles, she put on her swim cap to cover her short but thick orange hair. She wore silicone caps now because they lasted longer than the latex ones of her childhood. Her goggles had a metallic coating, great for acting as sunglasses during her lake swims, but not as useful for dungeonesque pools. She wondered if she still had a pair of Swedish goggles tucked away in an old swim bag. They only cost about five dollars and you could tailor the straps and nose piece to fit your face. The lenses had no padding so the narrow plastic edge rested around your eye sockets, often causing deeper goggle marks than other brands. That's why the other girls never wore them. Even if she could find an old pair, the straps would have either melted into the pocket in which she left them or would be so brittle they would crack into flakey pieces in her hands.

She and July were always the ones who jumped in and started warm ups right away while the other girls fretted about how cold the water would be or made unnecessary adjustments to their goggles. As an adult, in her lake, she walked in up to her waist then hopped off the sandy bottom to dive the rest of her body underwater, which, in the winter at least, was colder than the pool water.

So why was she hesitating now? Why didn't she just jump in like she always did? Feel the thrill of the tiny bubbles rise and explode on her skin until she moved fast enough not to notice them anymore. Was it the ache in her lower back? Was it real or did she imagine it now in anticipation of the flip turn? Would she even remember how to do a flip turn? It's like riding a bike, Ollie told her. It'll come back to you.

Maisie's eye flicked to the lifeguard on duty, a bored teenager sitting in a collapsible chair at the other end of the pool. He yawned and then inspected the dirt under his fingernails. Did he have what it took to rescue her if the flip turn took her out like it had done twenty years ago?

Maybe this was good enough, she thought, just to be here. And maybe next time she would get in and swim. Baby steps. Isn't that what the doctors and physical therapists had been telling her for years?

She took off her goggles and cap and stood up. She heard Ollie say, "I thought you were the adventurous one? Who are you?" And Maisie could only imagine the expression on July's face if she saw Maisie leaving the pool now. July always thought Maisie could/would do anything. If she were there, July would say something like, "Wow, crazy Maisie's getting lazy."

"Fuck off, Ju-Ju Bee," Maisie said under her breath. She sat down on the kickboard again and put her cap and goggles back on.

Ode to Husband as Fanatic

Praise
for the whole-
hearted and die-
hard, nit-picky
in passion, particular
in palm-waving for—
not music, but the ride 'em high
and low of jazz;
not baseball,
but the drive 'em long and far
and give up the field
for the Fenway Faithful;
not grilling,
but the turn 'em, the sauté
and never burn 'em—
steak and onions in heat wave;
shish-kabobs in blizzards;
asparagus wrapped tightly
in fresh during unexpected
April sleet.
And praise
for semi-secret societies
and secret-concoction salmon;
for the sacred and oft-venerated
grill covers, sweatshirts, coats,
mittens, blankets, pillows, light
switches, lamps, flags, signs,
ornaments, jewelry, keyboards, flash
drives, coffee cups, salt shakers,
shoelaces, socks of Red Sox
and Weber logos welcoming
each sunrise with aficionado
and bravo!
And, all hail
the well-lighted photo-shoot
of Thanksgiving turkey,

Christmas prime rib;
the smoky sanctity of beans,
but also the daily devotion to god-
forsaken grammar, to teaching,
to sound and sense and the recipe
of story served up as appetizer
or sit-down full course
as preparation for conversation:
baseball, grilling, God—
all serenaded by Thelonious.
O sing loud
the layered song of sentences
entwining tale and taste,
the last play and Last Supper,
smoky incense swirling up
toward the patron saint
of selective loyalty: you
who savor liturgy over
spontaneous prayer;
missal rhythms over
Xeroxed praise song,
your chant (acceptable
substitute for Coltrane)
always Gregorian.
So glory be
to God and hot coals,
to home runs, to late-night
jams, to Holy Days, to you
of the fierce beliefs,
who loves not every
song, team, grill,
ritual, person, just
one, just fan-of-you,
just me.

Marjorie Maddox

The Yellow Spikes

Dariusz Janczewski

The lime-yellow running spikes, my companion from many yesterdays, landed on my office desk like gloves discovered after a move from cold climates to the tropics: out of place, out of the comfort zone. Annoying but at the same time strangely beguiling.

They had been lying on my desk for several days. They looked unimposing, oblivious, probably tired, maybe disappointed, surely heartbroken. I put them there, after organizing the garage, because I was at a loss what to do with them. The plan was to while away the tidying ups and savor the memories of the long-time ago. It was time for the resurrection. They reappeared, and, due to my hopscotch pattern of life, maybe for the last time in my life, they were once again an object to cherish.

Stashed in the garage with other unwantables, they persisted for over thirty years, until I unpacked them from the other junk. You know that ambiguous instinct about clinging to the things we are unable to part with. One day—I thought—I can do something with them. Sooner or later (usually later), a few days after the clean-up, they would end up in the street's disposal bin and then be promptly taken away to the dump, by the trash collecting lorries.

There was not much left of the once diligently built sandcastle, except for the barely-possible-to-apprehend silicon grains of the fragmentary memories. The running spikes knew, as well as I did, that the trumpets of the won battles, and the drums of the lost ones, have long been silenced. My bones were more breakable, and my muscles were much less defined. My heart had been repaired and now was better than before, but still prone to melancholic musings. There were the round and heavy medals, awarded to me for winning races. They huddled in a cardboard box, somewhere in the garage's forgotten territories, and each time I thought about them, my recollections of the races won rolled back to me. And a pile of several flat, but warped by time, black and white photographs were strangely impervious and pretended to imitate the images of a younger me. Each time I clenched a handful of these unforgettable memories, they quickly and easily slipped between my fingers. Even my competitive edge, once the most potent energy perpetuating my days, had not been as athletic as before. But believe me, it still had a long way to go before it was completely beat. Those visual mnemonics alone had kept these ascending memories alive. Or so I thought, until the spikes had showed up. Their vivid reappearance once again exhilarated my long and inactive need to feel triumphant.

The racing spikes were odd things, who couldn't help but reclaim their place in my life. The transtemporal impostors, they planted themselves among my papers and books asking to be indulged in again. They were in a category by themselves. They lingered in the garage, hoping for someone to pick them up, put them on, lace them up, and start running—sorry, wrong number.…

The spikes couldn't possibly remember the banked, wooden indoor track in Warsaw, sometime in the winter of 1973. It was long before their time. I did not own them yet. Their predecessors were heavy and run-of-the-mill. They had a quarter of an inch tough rubber soles, four half-of-an-inch permanently set-in metal spikes in each forefoot, and stiff, white leather tops which were tied up with black shoelaces. I did not know anything better. I ran in what was given to me by my coach. I was happy and content, because I had been racing and winning more races than I had lost. Recording in my training journal all my victories, my failures, and my racing times—sometimes in tenths of a second— was a religion to me. I was a precocious fifteen-year-old, and at that time I had been training for less than two years. The indoor track that I ran on during that winter, in Warsaw, had four lanes. The track was an elongated oval 200 meters long in circumference, which was comprised of two 50-meters-long, steeply banked turns at each end of the two 100-meters-long flat and straight tracks connecting the curves. From a distance, its dark red wooden top looked smooth and shiny. But when I got closer, I saw that it was peppered with tons of pinholes, and splinters, made over the years by the runners' spikes. Like any gym, it smelled of wood polish. I was there to run the race; the spikes were there to do the damage—it was their job.

There must have been at least ten of us in the 800-meter race. I was not one of the favorites to win it. I was still unknown—a small town boy, with more dreams than ambitions. After the starter's gun, I took a safe position at the end of the pack. My coach had recommended it. He said: I know you are good, but today they are better—you are not there yet. Just stay near the end, and wait for the last lap, then go, and finish as strong as you can. And that was what I did.

I positioned myself at the end of the group and I waited. We had completed three laps and I heard the loud bell; it alerted us that we only had one more lap to go. And the most unexpected thing happened: I found myself in front of the race, with no one ahead of me, just the empty track. The drums of the runners' feet, pounding the wooden track ahead of me, went silent. I could only hear my own footsteps. The loud cheers of the excited coaches, and the yelling of the animated spectators, who densely surrounded the parameter of the track, went silent as well. The leader of the race had slipped on the steeply banked curve of the track and fell. Everyone who closely followed behind him tripped on his prostrated body, and fell as well. Being in the very back, I had just enough time to pass around the pile of runners whose limbs were waving like crabs picked out of the water—their eyes wide and confused. My instinct to accelerate kicked in a split second before I could grasp what had just occurred. But they were soon on their feet and back in the race. Adrenaline was flipping up their now invigorated wings. I could hear them behind, getting closer and closer to me. When I got to the final 30 meters of the race, I forced myself to use my arms, and I ran even harder. I didn't look to my sides, I just focused on my speed and the sight of the finish line ahead. I won the race. After I crossed the finish line, I stopped and waited for the other runners to end the race. I then shook their hands—congratulating every one of them. For me, it was never about winning, it was about competing. Smiles ran across their faces as they patted me on my shoulder. My first ever big race was a lesson of the you-never-knows…. And there were many of those, believe me: life did not prepare us for bizarre solutions. Did I feel guilty? No. I felt lucky—I still do. But, being with me for so long, the spikes must have already known that. I didn't know whatever became of those first spikes. They were probably either gifted by my coach to a new runner, or simply disposed of.

But they should remember those glorious and most vibrant days of our being part of the Polish National Team, where I would collect handshakes with Olympians like Bronisław Malinowski, Jacek Wszoła, Władysław Kozakiewicz, or John Walker. Was there any use to remind the spikes that my time as a national team runner was over? And that, consequently—if naturally—so was theirs? Did I have to bring to their attention the fact that, along with me, they had traveled across the ocean, on the plane, to another country, another continent, and that our journeys were over and done with? Yes, we were once as one. But I must have made it clear to them that I would never again be able to represent the nation which I could no longer represent. That I was not able to run that fast anymore—except in my dreams. I was a middle-aged man, and I was not interested in competition of any kind. I was tired of travels and of the rat race. I was sick of the lifestyle, which consisted of not much more than traveling, sleeping in the hotels, eating, and training three times a day. If I did not make it clear to them that we were simply done with all that nonsense, I was doing it now.

So, what's the point? And how about them, my newly recaptured running spikes. I did not know what happened to the rest of my national team uniform. But the truth be told, I have seriously, if profusely, outgrown all of it anyway.

The spikes were with me in the cars, buses, trains, and airplanes; always at the bottom of my duffle bag; blanketed by sweats, running jerseys, and other clothing. They always waited patiently to be put on, so we could chase the wind; sometimes as fast as under four minutes a mile—how many pairs of shoes, I wondered, have ever accomplished a feat like that? They were travelers with a cause. And they were still there, on my desk.

Their tops were made of a breathable lime-yellow mesh, and their sides were enforced by same-color suede. Vertical, plastic stripes—three on each side of each shoe's middle part—were powder blue. The plastic Achilles protectors were in the same blue and extended two inches above the heels of the spikes. The shoe-maker's logo was printed on them—the logo used to be bright gold, now it was a faded brown. The color of shoelaces closely matched the yellow hue of the exterior mesh. The back parts of the spikes' soles were made of a thin hard blue plastic, notched into a texture of sharp, tiny cuts. The forefeet of the spikes' soles recalled the aspect of dinosaurs' backs: they were bright yellow and had randomly dispersed, sharp, hard plastic cones and wedges. In-between the cones, and the edges, round, crown-like nests hosted metal spikes. Each shoe had six spikes screwed into threaded sockets. They were 1/8 of an inch-long spikes made for racing on a hard, tartan-surfaced track.

A question had to be asked: again, what's in store for them? Like my skin, and my face, they got older, duller, and weaker; afraid, squeamish about facing the unsurmountable, and daring the unthinkable—interested in much lower stakes. They used to epitomize my thick skin; share with me my mask of invincibility, and accompany me on my flying carpet, which kept transporting me to far-away lands. They were my Mercury, my mediator between me and the gods of victory. Now, it was up to me to decide the spikes' fate.

Many years ago, when I was just a boy, I would never have dreamed about competing in the same race with the New Zealand world record holder, Johnny Walker. And here I was—or rather, here we were, the spikes and me—standing next to the tall runner: all muscles, wrapped in Olympic confidence, a living legend, the god of middle-distance racing. He sported long blond hair, which fanned his kiwi black jersey and was adorned with an aboriginal necklace.

On the starting line of the 1500-meter race, we stood head-to-head, elbow to elbow, leg to leg, and spike to spike, waiting for the starting gun to explode and get us on our way. Thousands of spectator voices, in Budapest's sold-out stadium, thundered with cheers, as we took off and started circling the bright red tartan track. It was bathed in halogen lights, flourishing way up above everything, and making the stadium look brighter than daylight. There were at least a dozen runners in the race: some Hungarians, an Englishman, a couple of Americans (Steve Scott was there too), the fabulous New Zealander, and one Pole—me. I ran close to John Walker. But all I was able to take away from the race was the memory of his sweaty neck and a bouncing amulet around it. He, and a few of the others—also world-class runners—were out of touch. I took either the ninth or the tenth place in the race, clocking my personal best. Each time I remembered that event, I knew that I was not there to beat the Olympians; I was there to conquer the specter of my miserable childhood. I reckoned that all of us, the runners, had something in our lives to overcome, or to prove. Otherwise, why would we even bother to choose to practice this lonely, primal sport called running? And when we were done, we took off our spikes, and shook each other's hand. We were glad to have the race behind us, we would take the running spikes off, put them back in our duffle bag, and put the running shoes on.

I knew that the spikes understood what I was talking about. They rested on the desk by the books, now jealous about the novels being endowed with their own narrative closures. The spikes waited for their stories to be told. I admired them. I paid more attention to their presence after I had unearthed them in the garage than I had when they were in their limelight. Because, on the day of their sudden rebirth, they were not the objects of intermittent necessity anymore: now the spikes were the substance of my undivided attention and proud of their glorious moniker. Like a legend, a fable, or a myth, their unexpected reappearance had activated my terrestrial reveries. But their brass was faded, and their look mired in sweat and overuse. They were useless, and all they could do was to wait and learn about my intentions.

What's good about having the running spikes around after their usability had expired? Most of my running buddies had been removed from my life a long time ago. They were replaced by friends who didn't care about running, who liked to drink beer or hard liquor, and who had been reading philosophy or books by Joseph Conrad. They were renounced, put away like books already read; their lives reduced to anecdotal summaries. But the spikes might have asked me if, maybe, I wouldn't mind placing them behind a glass box and label them as valuable mementos? Just like Jessie Owens's spikes, for example. Or, how about rock stars' guitars in the museums: still playable, but no longer being played. The guitars were objects of fetish for the nostalgia-fed melancholics, who were neither able to forget the past nor wanted to remember it. That day, I was torn apart like the spikes.

All that we went through together. Were they some of the best times of my life? I am willing to admit that they were. But there were also times that I would rather not bring up anymore. And how about them, the spikes? I was willing to guess that the running times were the most memorable period of their lives. But what of it? Why would I want to linger on ancient history? History had taught us that we are never able to learn anything from the past. More than that: we kept making our mistakes repeatedly. We were all pitiful! Why would I want to remember my mistakes from the past? "Would you trust me," I said to them, "if I told you that the present has so much more to offer than the past? Plus, I was never a rock star—you know that, because neither were you— nor should we dare to compare ourselves to Jessie Owens!" Placing the spikes behind a glass cabinet would be too painful to contemplate: the past. Because I am willing to bet that they have never forgiven me for digging my own grave on that summer evening, in 1983, when I decided to be a pacesetter.

Sopot. The Polish seaside resort. Because it was protected from the winds by a wreath of closely planted trees, the track was one of the fastest in the country. When I had decided to set the pace in the race, I had no idea that my choice could result in the suicide of my running career. I was still unsure about it the day I had laid my eyes on you, in the garage. But the more I thought about it, the more I looked at the pace-setting adventure from the perspective of a sculptor: to me, it was always child's play with unlimited possibilities. On that warm summer day in Sopot, in 1983, you were with me.

A day before the race, the coach of the runner who was the favorite to win had approached me with a proposition to be a pacesetter. There was money to be made. He was very nice to me—he had never been so nice to me either before the race or afterwards. The true scope of his personality had not become apparent to me until many years later, when I matured, philosophically speaking. For my volunteering to be the pacesetter for his pupil, he had offered me what at that time of my life had seemed like a huge amount of money. Not knowing any better—not being able to grasp the ramification of my hasty decision—I had accepted the coach's offer. Pleasing people had always been my weakness. For a couple of weeks before the race, I had been in the best running shape of my life. I knew this from the workouts: I had run the quarter mile and half-mile repeats faster than ever before. I wanted to run even more repeats and had to be stopped by my coach. He had known better than to tire me out at the workouts: "If you want to show me how good you are," he had said, "do it during the upcoming race in Sopot." I had never remembered how I had spent that money, but I would never forget how I had made it.

The other coach's proposition was simple and straight forward: as soon as the 1500-meter race started, I was to take the lead, and run in a record-setting pace. I was to keep the lead for the initial three (out of the three and a three-quarters) laps, so his runner—and the other runners participating in the race—could just stay close behind me and thus not worry about losing precious energies because of tactical shuffling. All that was needed of them was to follow me closely and, during the last three hundred meters of the race, sprint to the finish; hopefully, in a record-setting time. When my pace-setting part of the race was done after three laps, I was to either step off the track, or move away from its inside lane, so the runners behind me could pass unobstructed. Since I had collected my pay a day before the race, there was nothing more to it.

It was a perfect evening in Sopot. The wind was out to sea, barely perceivable because of the track-engulfing pine trees. Still hot from the earlier sun, the red and bouncy tartan track was buzzing with activity. The announcer's low voice could be heard coming from the speakers. The sprinters were darting by, and the long jumpers were leaping forth. At the distant end of the stadium, the shot put and discus throwers were spinning in their rings before releasing their projectiles. The pole vaulters were balancing on the tips of their rods, feeling the faint breeze of cool sea air gliding above the stadium's tree line. Occasional yelps or shouts of the coaches and the spectators completed the soundscape. The stadium was surrounded on three sides by metal bleachers, mostly occupied by athletes. They either rested before their events or recuperated after. A few townsfolk, keen on track and field, were picnicking on blankets which they had spread on the grassy mounds behind the bleachers. They came to watch the country's best athletes, hoping to witness a record-breaking performance.

The 1500-meter race that was about to start could be one of the record-setting races. The race began, and as arranged, I took the lead and I started setting the pace. After two laps, our half-mile split was 1 minute and 53 seconds. I was running roughly at a pace which, theoretically speaking, could result in 3 minutes and 36 seconds finishing time—over three seconds faster than my personal best in the event. Naturally, my coach was in the dark about my decision to become a pacesetter. And now I could see and hear him jumping from the bleachers and onto the track, and yelling at me: "What are you doing? Slow down!" But it was too late. We were already approaching the last three hundred meters of the race. It was time for me to either drop out, or to move to the right, and make space for the runners behind to start/finish line. But I didn't. Despite the very fast pace, I knew that I was not spent, so I kept racing. On the last stretch, I was passed by the runner whose coach convinced me to become the pacer. I still finished in second place and clocked the second fastest time I ever ran in that event. I had been in much better shape than I thought I was. Had I known better, I might had even won the race.

And the spikes certainly do remember the emigration; the time in refugee camp, and the college days—there were still some active years for them, even though I was already starting to put my trophies away, collect the old photographs in photo albums which I rarely opened, and stuff the unwantables somewhere where they would collect dust. I got up and picked the spikes up from the messy desk. I looked at them closely. They were almost weightless, like memories. I could probably put them on my feet right now, and they would still fit me. They were ominously silent. And an idea hit me: I was in need of feeling the spikes on my feet again. I felt strangely sprightly and excited. Was that how I felt, more than thirty years ago, when I was about to put them on my feet before the races?

The shoelaces kept the pair of the racing spikes tied together. I undid the knot and separated them. Handling one shoe at a time, I looked inside them. There was mouse poop inside. I went back to the garage and threw away the nasty droppings. Small debris fell out of them like beads of the calcified past. I washed my hands with soap and then grabbed a rag, so I could wipe the dust from the exteriors, and the interiors, of the shoes. I went back to my office and sat down on a chair by my desk. I took my socks off and started massaging my bare feet. I used to do this before each race.

I began with the left shoe. I picked it up and I immediately felt the dust on my fingers. Carefully and thoroughly, I wiped the dirt off the spikes with the rag. Next, I started to expand the shoe's interior, by first loosening the laces and then expanding the sides with my hand. I examined the shoe's interior more carefully. It was like looking inside of a make-believe cave from childhood, after many years of absence; familiar but missing the consciousness of innocence; dirtier and bleaker, less apologetic than the memories of it. I took the shoe and gently twisted its body, checking for its flexibility. I felt a slight resistance. One more loosening move with my hands, to expand the shoe's interior, and my left foot went in. But only halfway: I instantly realized that I needed to loosen the laces even more. I did it quickly and skillfully with my two index fingers—old habits die hard. Like old stitches, the yellow laces emitted a slight screeching sound. This time the foot went in. After a few seconds, it became painfully clear to me that the shoe was too small. My foot did enter the shoe, but it stretched its fabric so much that the interior of the shoe, where the arch of my foot was, looked like a side of a tent. The foot's toe knuckles were bulging at the front of the shoe, as if the shoe was filled with pebbles. There was no reason to try: either the shoe was too small, or the foot too swollen. Maybe both of us got too old? To relieve the discomfort—and embarrassment—I took the shoe off my foot without even attempting to lace it up.

"I am sorry to make you go through this," I said. Then, after almost giving up on the exercise, I decided to try on the other shoe: I must be fair, I thought. Something occurred to me: During a track race, the right spike is always at a disadvantage. Because the runners run on the track in a counterclockwise manner, the right leg is always on the outside of the track's inner curb. The right-foot spike has to run a slightly longer distance than the left spike—one spike is perpetually working harder than the other. The right spike needed to get its chance as well.

I went through the same procedure as I did with the left spike and started to loosen up the laces of the right shoe. I put the right foot in, and then I quickly took it out. The spike shared the faith of its twin brother: Did aging make people bigger? Did shoes contract with age? What's the point? I thought. Yes, we did try, on so many occasions! But not anymore. True, sometimes we failed, but often we were victorious. I got up, and I put the spikes back on the desk.

I was ready to make a quick and unequivocal decision to banish the spikes from my life. I looked at them again. Then I picked them up and went to my dresser located in the nearby bedroom. I changed into my jogging shorts and a t-shirt. I put on my sneakers and walked outside. It was late September and my wife, Katie, was harvesting the ripe vegetables, ready to be picked from our garden before the winter weather set in. When she saw me, I told her that I was just going to the horse trailhead to do something very important. She looked and saw that I had my old running spikes in my hand. She smiled at me and nodded, as if she understood what I was up to.

The horse trailhead was just across the street from our house in Montana, and in the evenings, it was almost always empty, except for some very few in-between hikers. I grabbed the spikes as I always did—with one hand, two of them, sole to sole—and started toward the trail. As I expected, nobody was there. I walked to one of the two boulders that designated the entrance to a secondary trail and circumvented the trailhead, and I sat on the bigger one. I took my sneakers off, and I put on my spikes. Again, they felt uncomfortably small on my feet. I got up and started jogging on the flat, loose gravel-covered trail.

The trail was next to the Forest Service information board that displayed a large map of the Rattlesnake Recreational Area, as well as a few fliers warning about black bears frequenting the area. The gravel under my feet made familiar cracking noises. I jogged for about thirty yards, now and then looking down at my spiked feet. I was in control of my cadence and monitoring proper form of my arms and legs. I breathed evenly. I then turned around and ran back toward the boulders, but this time a little faster. I got back to my shoes, thought about stopping there, but I didn't. I again turned around, and I ran away from the boulders even faster than seconds before. Then, one more turnaround, and I sprinted back as fast as I could! I got to the rocks with my shoes, and ran past them, racing faster and faster—until I was out of breath. I stopped. I was beat. I walked toward the running shoes in the way I had always done after a race: right hand on my right hip, left arm down next to my side, my chin on my chest, head looking down. My breathing was hard, and I was recovering with each walking step. I moved my head from side to side in disbelief: the spikes did not feel too small anymore—they fit me like gloves. For a moment we were back in our element. I sat down on one of the boulders and untied the laces. I took the spikes off my feet, put my sneakers back on, and I got up. I picked the spikes up, looked at them, and I said: "Thank you." I placed them face to face, and I walked back home.

The next day, I laid the spikes gently on my desk. I returned the Vila-Matas' novella, which I was reading, where it belonged—with other literature books. All the pencils scattered over my desk went back into the jar where they always had been. The spikes just rested there, content and somehow more yellow. I again joined them by tying their laces together. I opened my office window shades, so the sunlight could enter. I took out my digital camera, which was always within my reach, and turned it on. I took several photos of the spikes; from different angles and from different points of view—I covered all the bases—and when I decided that I was done with taking the photographs, I took the spikes and placed them in a white shopping bag.

That afternoon I visited the Goodwill store on the distant side of town. I stopped my car in front of the drop off door and waited for assistance. A woman came out. "Hi," she said, "do you need a receipt for your donation?" she asked. I said "no." "Is this all you have?" she asked me, eyeing the meager size of my donation "Yes," I said, "that's it." She looked inside the bag I gave her, and then looked at me. "What are those?" she asked. "Those are called running spikes," I answered. "Oh," she said, clearly not understanding. She turned around and casually walked away toward the door where she came from. Then I saw her hand reaching out and getting ready to close the door behind her. I got out of the car, and I caught up with the spikes before they were forever gone. I had decided that my memories were more important to me than my future.

Post-Game

Nothing brings us down after a road win.
Popcorn stuck to our boots delights us.
Crossing the court floor's golden sea,
We shake their dolphin mascot's flipper.
A crushed popcorn box is stuck in his blowhole.
We pat his back and inquire about his breathing.
Inside is a five foot four freshman
Drowning in sweat, wheezing from a cold,
Needing to study for a geometry test.

Snowflakes swirl about our faces as we exit.
Air becomes pinched and tight down the steps.
We pull hats low and collars up.
Road home is long and winding.
Leaves and snow fog blow across.
A leaping buck nearly grazes our bumper.

Yet our chatter is long-running,
Approaching holy, and farcical.
We exit the truck cab,
While wind doesn't know what to do with us,
Slapping our faces to cheer us down,
And the front door, old curmudgeon,
Just glares and glares.

Thomas Reynolds

Morton's Toe

Jacob Cohen

This was before the internet. No Google, Yahoo!, or cell phones, so it's not like they could've really known who Coach Sliznowski really was. They found out the hard way about Coach. It wasn't until after the rivalry game that it all blew up. Only reason I found out was because JC told me the story after he got away. He checked in at the scorer's table.

"Can I get a sub on the next whistle?" JC said to the ref.

The referee nodded, whistle dangling on his lower lip. On the next whistle, he checked in for Ralph. Ralph could rebound with the best of them, but he was what Coach Sliznowski called slow footed. Coach Sliznowski, called Sliz or Slizzard by his team when he wasn't in earshot, knew JC wasn't the best shooter. On its face, it wasn't the oddest substitution in basketball history, but looking back on it, someone could've started getting curious right there. JC could guard anybody, big or small, and he had an uncoachable knack for stealing the ball and making a layup on the other end. Still, he couldn't shoot, especially a three pointer. Coach knew that, but he put him in anyway. The whole town knew Sliznowski had a propensity for rolling the dice. Rumor had it that he even bet on his own games in college. Some say he was persuaded by the local tough guys, but others still just said he couldn't resist a bet.

JC was sort of a fan favorite because he was always diving for balls and getting the crowd pumped up with his antics. A cheer of "JC" rang out when he checked in.

"JC, guard Sampson," coach Sliz instructed.

"Sampson? Who the hell is that?"

"Number 35," Coach said.

"But he's two inches taller than me," JC protested.

"You can handle it, kid."

The ref handed JC the ball. Their worst defender guarded JC. He made the inbound pass and got into position to run the offense. He was a pretty good ball handler and quick, so when he was in, he played point guard. JC fed Aaron who scored on a jumper from the wing. The score was tied. The gymnasium shook back and forth and the crowd chanted, "Let's go Defense!" Brookline called a timeout.

They were in the hands of Sliz now. He relished timeout pep talks. Figured he could get more out of his guys through motivation, than drawing some circles and arrows that just looked like hieroglyphics. The team may have had nicknames for him, but he had earned his stripes with them and they played for him, not in spite of him. He had played college ball in Brooklyn at St. Francis. Sliznowski loved the game. I wasn't even on the team, but you could just tell. Coach liked to ride guys a bit too much sometimes, but JC said it made you have thick skin and he was just trying to squeeze every ounce of talent out of their scrawny bodies. He almost played semi-pro, but he broke his ankle playing street ball and was never the same player or person. Still, his desire to win was contagious and his teams generally won under that spell. He knelt down and had the obligatory clipboard and dry erase marker, but he didn't draw any arrows or circles. He had something to say.

"No matter what, you guys are my favorite team of all time. Coached a lot of kids over the years and forgot most of their names and one day I'll forget yours too. But you guys? You guys are a team. Go win or go lose. Really doesn't matter, but we all gotta be on board."

There followed an awkward silence and an unspoken confusion amongst them. JC sensed this and after a few seconds rolling it around in his head and mustering up the courage, he spoke up.

"What do you want us to run out there, Coach?" JC asked.

But the Slizzard didn't answer him. The other guys sort of echoed in mumbles to offer support of this question, but he didn't answer them either. They broke the huddle with no strategy or direction. This was to go to the state Championships and play at the Garden in Boston. If Newton North won, it'd have been the first time playing on the parquet floors of the infamous Boston Garden.

The ref blew the whistle for a few seconds too long. Perhaps indicating his desire for this game to be over with.

Brookline inbounded with thirty seconds hanging on the clock. As soon as the ball made contact with the receiver, the clock would start. Brookline could do two things with the possession. Run the clock down and hold the rock for a final shot, or zip down the court and try to score as soon as possible. The latter strategy was an attempt at securing a second shot, should the opponent score on their shot and leave time left on the clock. Brookline decided to go with the two-score approach and got the ball in quick and blazed down the floor.

JC had decided to guard their point guard. Like himself, this guy had some handle and was not slow footed. JC tried to stay with him stride for stride, but this time he was a step too slow and Brookline hoisted a two point lead and only shed seven seconds from the clock. Sliznowski popped out from his chair like a Jack-in-the-Box toy and signaled timeout. Once again, they sat around him looking for a grain of sage wisdom to drop from his mouth.

"We got the time. Twenty-three seconds, but Jesus, why'd you let them score without a fight?"

He was staring at JC. Public shame was a favorite tool of the Sliz and JC responded particularly well to that form of punishment, not wanting to be at fault for the group's failures.

"Wasn't like I didn't run with him. I didn't want to put him on the line either," JC said.

Coach skipped over that reply and moved into strategy mode.

"Ok, let's not piss this away. We need a three pointer. Screw overtime, it's not happening. We either win by one or lose by two. Understand?"

They just nodded. It wasn't clear who was supposed to be taking the final shot. There were a couple decent options, but the long ball was not their strength. Brookline knew this and would have given them ample room to launch a shot up from deep. They knew Slizzard liked to roll the dice. From five dollar scratch offs to hundred dollar exacta boxes at Saratoga, he was always betting on something. This time he was betting on them and none of them knew it until later.

They got the ball inbounded without much pressure. JC took the ball from Keith, the team's tallest guy at 6'4", and looked up to peek at the clock, taking in the fact they only had 19 seconds left. He surmised the only thing he could do was dribble until there was only a few seconds left. Then he'd either find an open man for the final shot, or be forced to heave it up himself. He dribbled to the left wing and tried to cross over and go right. Suddenly, he was double-teamed. Usually, he could navigate out of such a situation, but this time he was flummoxed. He didn't want to pull a Chris Webber and call a timeout they didn't have, so he tried to draw a foul. It worked. The ref raced over to help JC up. 10 seconds left. He wanted to inbound the ball and pass to someone who could shoot. He found Aaron again and instantly he drew the double team. Aaron reacted appropriately, making a bounce pass back to JC. There were only five seconds left. He had to take the shot.

After the game, Coach Sliznowski was nowhere to be found. The team was bull-rushed to the floor by the crowd and swallowed. Local police scampered across the floor to untangle the puzzle of cheering fans. Before they entered the locker room, they were held back by the yelling between Coach and this guy named Archie.

"You told me that kid couldn't shoot. He hit nothing but net. What an asshole you are."

"I can't swat the ball away. I'm just a coach."

"Screw all that. Bottom line is you owe me money. You said it was a lock."

"Money? I don't have any money. I'm a goddamn high school basketball coach."

"No, what you are is a bum."

"Look, I don't got the money. And I'm not gonna have it anytime soon."

They heard the whole thing. Supposedly, Coach Sliz had guaranteed Archie they'd lose. He put JC in so that would happen, hoping that the last shot was going to be taken by him. After that, they couldn't hear any more arguing. Archie must've knocked him out. Maybe with a gun or the butt of his knife. The one he used to slice off Coach Sliznowski's Morton's toe. Once they heard the screaming, the fellas rushed in. Archie had backup they hadn't anticipated. Two goons that were mutes. They must've been bodyguards or something. The team froze and most of them got beat up pretty bad, but like I said, JC got away and told me about it all later on.

When the guys dug into it a little further, they found out a whole bunch about Coach and his playing days and gambling days. Sometimes all you had to do was poke around and you could uncover a thing or two, that would lead into another thing or two. Coach Sliznowski had Morton's toe which he never really talked about. After one of his prep school games, he found out he had it. He was in the locker room undressing after a victory when his teammate yelled out:

"Holy shit, you got Mo Mo toe. I've heard about it and all, but I've never actually seen it. Only on statues on stuff."

"What the hell is Mo Mo toe?" Stephen Sliznowski asked.

"Technically, it's Morton's toe. It's when your second toe is larger than your big toe, moron."

Everyone laughed, but Sliznowski just kinda got lost looking at his toe, as if for the first time. He looked it up later on and started studying all the paintings and sculptures that had Morton's toe in it. He even went to see "The Boxer." He felt honored to have the toe and even theorized that he was quicker because of it. After games in college, he would brandish the toes after games to the amusement of friends and fans alike. It was a way to stand out, no matter how small. Anyway, Archie caught wind of Sliznowski's affinity for his toes. That's why he plucked them from his feet when Sliznowski protested and refused to make good on his faulty guarantee about the game.

Later on, when the guys would see Coach Sliznowski on the street or in the grocery store, he had special shoes outfitted to support his feet and he walked with an awful limp from side to side. He rarely was seen out after a few years of enduring the stares and whispers of the town. After the incident, there was a bunch of investigations and interviews, but nothing came of it. Coach was more ashamed that he was betting on his own kids to lose than anything else.

He could justify betting on them to win, but the fact that he tried to throw the game was repulsive, even to him. He never coached again.

The team went on to the State Championships and lost in the Boston Garden to Roxbury. The game wasn't even close as they had two future Division One prospects and a slew of Division Two guys. After the Brookline game, JC's confidence ballooned and he started throwing up three pointers with abandon and sinking a good amount of them. He was starting to get recruited and make some noise around town. Once in a while, you'd catch Coach Sliznowski hanging out at the park watching the guys play basketball in the summer. He never breached the invisible line he'd created to come over and talk to us, but we all knew he was there. JC wasn't mad or anything, but he was glad he scored the shot. Even if Coach Sliz lost his Morton's toes.

Credo in Deum

That impossible shot
from full fucking
court that has us
both frozen
in our seats as it arcs
through the air
and even the shooter
doesn't understand
how it's left his hand,
a miraculous heave
that combines perfect
desire and precision,
leaving me to think
one can live
a lifetime without
seeing this, yet here
it is, unbelievable,
undeniable,
and I'll be able
to recall the rest
of my days
that soundless sound
on the far end,
followed by a crisp,
soulful swish,
and the joyful crowd
and shouts pouring out
of you, out of me
when simultaneously
we both leap to our feet

and the ball goes in,
the ball comes out,
drops down,
kisses hardwood,
and right then,
exulting en masse,
I turn to you, almost
tell you that if you
can give me something
as beautiful, improbable
as this, I might be able
to pretend finally
to believe
in your God.

Albert Haley

A Mere Glance

Jeffrey Wald

What does one second have to do with eternity? Surely they can't last, these moments dropped like pennies in the grass, never to be sought. Never to be found again. That's all they are; the past; passed and gone; gone and dead; only existing now as phantoms in the brain. But they too shall be buried under six feet of dirt and dusted then covered in snow, frozen in time, only existent in the past. Right?

It started merely as a glance, eyes connecting across the table, communicating—perhaps nothing. Perhaps there was nothing in the glance, only chance. But we seemed to linger there, a second, perhaps even two. And in that space—that temporal, finite, limited space—potentiality arose. Potentiality unbound by space and time, unbound by the present bounds of this dinner conversation, in this alien city, hearing the mindless chatter and feeling the shot clock counting down—three, two, one—until I can excuse myself and go away, up to Room 333 to watch SportsCenter on perpetual repeat, listening to Dan Patrick ask again and again and again *will the Bulls ever be good again.*

Damn the red-hot molten lava that spews and shoots and gushes, flowing unbound down, melting all within its path, unseeing, until it hits the sea and hisses, hisses and cools, cools and remains, like a wound, like a keloid scar. If the mind has mountains, it is an active volcano, molten. Red.

It was just a glance. That one second cannot, should not, mean anything more than any other second that I've lived before. And yet. Michael took 29,034 shots in his career. Not to mention the thousands of millions of billions of practice shots. Each day. Each and every day. Each release less than a second. Each of equal significance. Each a mere flick of the wrist. A letting go. A release.

And a mere glance to see *did it go in*. Such a shot on a Wednesday afternoon on a concrete court in 1975 in Wilmington as significant as the shot June 14, 1998 at the Delta Center. Right right right?

I arise and say goodnight, set my dirty napkin on the plate, turn around without another glance, and step inside the flight. I push the number "3," the symbol of perfection, harmony, and wisdom (like the three-pointer, the three-peat, and Dennis, Scottie, Michael); also of time, past present future; beginning middle end; birth life and death. The mind has tracks, like an elevator shaft; push the stone down the hill and it shall gather no moss, but it may kill the goat grazing down below.

The door was closing, would have closed, shut, altered time, but for, but for. But for the slender painted hand that slipped between the gap between the what is and the what could be. The what shall be.

And then another glance.

And a ding.

And four feet emerging from the shaft.

This couldn't last. This silent tension. This pulsing, throbbing tension in the mind, the throbbing piping of my inner self, sending crimson fluid from my beating core to all my limbs, descending, ascending, this crimson fluid the same color as her painted lips.

And then we find ourselves outside my door.

Looking down the name tag reads "Lenore."

Soon our clothes lie crumpled on the floor.

It began with a glance. Our eyes meeting for one second. But one second in this lonely, lonely world of ours marks the beginning of eternity.

Or does it?

I can't decide whether one second means everything, or nothing. Perhaps I am a sad, sad fool; looking for meaning where there is none. Hearing the eloquent raven when others block their ears at the caw, caw, cawing of the crow. Maybe the tale told by the idiot is a tale told by me.

I have not seen the crimson lips since. Though I haunt the place from time to time, order shrimp and calamari and $100 bottles of wine, just waiting for a glance, ride in the elevator shaft to Room 333 and lie upon my bed looking at that spot on the ceiling, that red dot, that same one I looked at then, no larger than a ladybug, listening to endless repeats of SportsCenter and waiting for the countdown, "11, 10" and then the call, "Jordan a drive, hangs, fires, Yes! Scooooores!!" The crimson red jerseys, the crimson red jerseys. I can see it in my mind. One second. One measly, tiny, particulate. But Michael now eternal. Michael now immortal.

But my seconds, my seconds, my seconds, drip away like a leaky faucet.

I close my eyes now. But all I see is red.

I close my eyes now, lying on this bed.

I close my eyes now, wishing I were …

But then a ding from my phone, that calls me back to that elevator shaft.
Pick it up and give it a worthless glance. But glancing back are the words
Not *nevermore.*
But I am *with child.*
Forevermore, forevermore, forever and forevermore.

*　*　*

I read these lines now and blush in embarrassment. It's not that the
words are untrue, or the tone false. I meant them when written; was struck by
what might be called poetic inspiration; was raised to the glorious heights of
visionary rapture. And I for one know that does not come often. Perhaps only
once or twice in one's entire lifetime. And those of us who have experienced
that burning fire know that there is nothing greater this world can offer. Which
is why when the great Hopkins wrote his last poem, titling it after that prick
and poser Robert Bridges, he wrote
Sweet fire the sire of muse, my soul needs this;
I want the one rapture of an inspiration.
For he knew also, as do I, that those inspirations are few and far between.
That most of our lives are as the expectant mother; waiting; longing; *nine
months … nay years.* Yes years. Years and years and years. Waiting for lightning
to strike, while we remain *haggard at the heart, so care-coiled, care-killed, so fagged,
so fashed, so cogged, so cumbered.*
Is all poetry false? A longing for bliss and awe and transfiguration that is
ultimately unachievable? The evocation of unfillable desire?
And yet, what I wrote was true; at least true for me when written. And
perhaps true for me even now. Although I don't yet know the ending. I guess
I'll have to wait and see if it's a happy one.

*　*　*

When I was a child, I had a terrible fear of letting people down; of folks
having their illusions about me shattered, revealing the quite ordinary, often
pathetic, self that is me. For instance, if I had a charming and flirtatious
conversation with a sweet lass, later, I would just about have a panic attack.
How can I repeat that performance, I would think to myself? I am not that
charming, that funny, that capable of carrying a conversation. Like George
Costanza who charms a beautiful woman while wearing a baseball cap, and
ever after is terrified to reveal his bald head to the woman. Terrified to, in a
sense, reveal his true self to the woman. I too would ever after go out of my way
to avoid these pretty girls lest they finally saw me for what I really was.
I wonder sometimes if this isn't why Michael quit when he did. How do you
top The Shot? Anything after—even another MVP and championship—would
be banal, ordinary, and expected. When you're a god, one expects miracles.

Paradox of paradoxes. Although my whole being ached for even a single glance from Lenore, moments after I received the text I sank into a paroxysm of doubt. It's not that I feared the longing I felt for Lenore might be dissembled and deconstructed; I had preserved an image of her in my mind of pure beauty. The golden skin. The raven hair. And the smile. Yes, that smile forever preserved in my memory, to be recalled and remembered at will. No, the problem was I had surely created an Illusion in Lenore's own mind. About who I was, and what I was capable of. And I knew I could not live up to that Illusion.

For that reason, the idea of marriage had always filled me with a sense of dread. Even though of a poetic nature, capable of donning masks and costumes as needed, how could I maintain a false face for a lifetime? And isn't that what marriage entails?

Thus, sitting there on the edge of that hotel bed, upon that floral-patterned comforter, my feet upon the green carpet, staring staring staring at the text message, I almost stood up and fled. Nearly ran out the door and onto the street to hide among the prostitutes and addicts that roamed the night. Afraid to recreate the fantasy. If Michael knew when to hang up the sneakers, might I not learn the same lesson? I alone of Bulls fans was secretly overjoyed when Michael retired after the 97-98 season. Michael the god, the dream, the Platonic Form, the sonnet in motion, had ended in perfection. Just as he should. No bad knees making him look old and pathetic. No cocky teenagers posterizing him. No paunchy midsection. Poets are meant to die young—Percy Shelley, John Keats, Sylvia Plath, Hart Crane, the list goes on—before they turn dour and bitter and nostalgic, bemoaning loss and death and collapse. By dying young, the poet paradoxically becomes immortal.

And Michael had done this, had become a poster hanging in the bedroom of every 10-year-old, Michael in mid-air, tongue out, flying over Ewing, time suspended forever. Or my own limited edition autographed photo hanging in my office of Michael floating like a piece of cotton, Russell looking up, whispering a prayer, the ball not yet released, a moment of suspense encased forever; we know what will happen, what does happen, but that moment one of pure possibility, pure potency. The fact that I have that picture, and not the one where the ball has landed in the net, perhaps reveals my psychosis. The preference for possibility over actuality. The dream versus reality. Poetry over prose.

But then, the Wizards. *The Wizards?* Are they even in the NBA? Horror of horrors. I couldn't watch; for two full seasons, I pretended the NBA was on strike, that Michael was still quietly retired hitting dimpled white balls on a golf course somewhere down south. But I knew I was living a lie.

* * *

Have you ever had to confront a fantasy in the flesh? Us dreamers—would-be poets the lot of us—are ever filled with illusions. The stream floats by, carrying leaves and twigs and silt from last night's storm and we see nothing. Content we are to live in the quiet and peace of our minds (yet that too is an illusion; the mind perhaps the island wracked most by storms).

But are illusions a bad thing? Even our crazed illusions, if left simply to fester in the imagination, cannot do that much damage; like Ahab pacing peg-legged on the deck; pacing pacing pacing. If he had never actually confronted Moby Dick, perhaps he'd still be pacing today. I grant you that maybe doesn't appear to be the greatest existence, but it's better than being swallowed by a whale. Right? I think Ahab was a poet, better left to illusions of revenge and glory and cosmic justice. And if he had remained in his illusions and never set sail on the Pequod to confront the Leviathan in the flesh, he would not have been swallowed up. The encounter with reality did him in.

Bullshit, you say, *I call bullshit*. It wasn't reality that did him in, but rather the idiotic illusion in the first place. The chicken or the egg. Half a dozen of one, six of the other.

But you might have a point. Perhaps I have given the impression that I am a poet. I am not a poet. I am an actuary. Go figure. But remember, Stevens was an insurance executive, and Eliot a Dickensian bank clerk. Knowing this, you proclaim: I smell hyperbole! You would-be wordsmith—tired of your numbers and Excel spreadsheets and deductions on the life span of a typical 39-year-old, obese Omahan with a penchant for sky diving—simply delight in the opportunity to wax poetic. To make your sad, pathetic existence contain a stroke of drama where none exists. You'd love to play the part of Edgar in *King Lear*, a minor part no doubt but at least a part (my name, by the way, is Edgar—you thought I liked Poe just for the heck of it?). By George, you'd play Steve Kerr if you could! But the sad fact is you're not even Doug McDermott. Your drama is invented.

I posit the possibility that you are correct; that I don't have a handle on my own illusions; that I am not aware of the many layers of my own self-consciousness. But let me ask you: what is the single most epiphanic experience you have ever had? That moment when meaning, purpose, reality emerged with clarity, like morning dew upon a daisy. When you beheld not merely the *thing*, but the thing behind the thing; the substance, the essence, the nub, the quiddity. Poet or not, we've all had them. Williams's red wheelbarrow. Hopkins's windhover. Dickinson's liquor never brewed. Peter at the Transfiguration. But what happens when you come down from that experience? Don't we all, like Peter, want to not come down? Let's build three tents! Stay here forever! But Jesus's reported response? *Get behind me Satan.*

Or what of Williams? Did he sit on his front steps beholding the red wheelbarrow all the rest of his days? Or, more likely, did his wife see him sitting there, daydreaming again, and yell out: *Damn it, William! The chicken poo is going nowhere so long as you stare at that old wheelbarrow!* So, Williams must arise, brush off his dusty pants, grasp the wheelbarrow, and go muck around in the chicken coop. Illusions quashed. A thick dose of reality the prescribed medicinal cure.

Oh Lenore, Lenore, Lenore! The blazing emerald eyes! The wild raven hair! The curves more pronounced than the Indianapolis Speedway's! You were my epiphany. You were my inspiration. If not a hack, I would have written the most perfect sonnet to you.

Paradox of paradoxes. My first meeting with Lenore, the single-most epiphanic experience of my life. And though my whole being screamed out for another encounter, to merely glimpse here again, or to smell the gentle fragrance of her shampoo as she passed by. I knew that the moment I did, *all would be lost*. Is it not impossible to exit a dream without waking up?

The word "lost" is poignant. For I was lost, with no hope of finding my way. Sitting on the edge of the bed (why do you keep going back, go forward man, go forward, get on with the story; forgive me, just this once, I can't help but repeat myself; remember, I am the one who has watched Game 6, 1998, *hundreds of times*), I knew if I never saw her again, my life would be an endless vinyl of loss, regret, and unmet desire. But on the other hand, if I *did* see her again, my life would be an endless Ferris wheel of loss, regret, and unmet desire. Damned if I do, damned if I don't. Stuck in a Beckett play either way.

So, I stopped thinking, and wrote the words *I want to see you again* and quickly pushed send. And off it went into cyberspace, like a rocket or a fired bullet, with no possibility of retrieval. I saw the text change from "r" (received) to "o" (opened). And I sat there in furious expectation. I wanted to look away but couldn't. Seconds ticked as an eternity. The shot clock going up, not down. 20, 21, 22. Then one minute. Idiot, idiot, idiot, I wanted to scream. Why did you do it? I knew this would never work out. And then I saw the little circle thing spinning, and the words *Lenore is typing a message.* And I stopped breathing (and perhaps my heart stopped beating) and then the words *The Starbucks on 5th and Grand. Tomorrow at 10?*

* * *

So it was that I found myself sitting at one of those mini tables at Starbucks, by turns staring into my iced caramel macchiato, spinning the cubes around, and then feverishly looking up toward the entranceway every time the bells jingled to a new arrival. Don't think it didn't occur to me that there was still time; a moment or two left to run; to flee; to hide. To lie on my bed and pull the covers over my head.

But then the doorbells jingled, and a waft of Chicago air blew the scent of Dove shampoo toward me, and I looked up, and she with glowing teeth, smiled. She smiled. And was I imagining it or did she ever so lightly place her hand upon her belly? I was perhaps imagining it, but it seemed, even now, so early, a blossoming. A growing fleshiness, and loveliness.

I will spare you the minutiae of our meeting (but don't think I didn't agonize and assess and decode it for weeks thereafter). I was prepared for my very being to unravel, like a baseball whose hide has been torn off. But it wasn't like that. I take no credit in that. Lenore, it turned out, was exceedingly normal, and natural, and capable of carrying the conversation. Sure, that same conversation progressed in fits and spurts, but Lenore kept it from devolving into extreme awkwardness. We simply got to know each other a little bit. I learned Lenore had been raised in Milwaukee, that she was one of three sisters, and that although she'd been offered a track scholarship at UW Madison, she didn't really care for sports. Instead, she studied Economics and History at the University of Chicago.

After 47 minutes, Lenore looked down at her watch, said something to the effect that she really must be going; one of those daily fires at Travelers needing to be put out before the lunch hour. I looked down at my half-eaten blueberry muffin, not knowing what to say. Not knowing what to do. And she said my name, Edgar, and calmly, exceedingly tenderly, said, *Look, thanks for this. It means a lot. Really it does. I'm glad we did this. But you don't have to. You made a mistake. This is now my burden to carry. You've got a life to live. You needn't be punished for one bad decision. Really, I'll be fine. My mother lives nearby. Don't be the martyr.*

Sometimes the unexpected happens. Sometimes we surprise even ourselves. Before I could think my way out of this, I blurted out, *But I want this. I want to make this work. I want to take care of our son.*

* * *

Six months later, I was in a delivery room at Northwestern Medicine, reality firmly and thoroughly thrust upon me. Sweaty, panting, laboring reality. How many love poems have ever been written, filled with sweet and tender whispers, moonlit forbidden embraces, and desperate longing, the fulfillment of which makes the heart cry out? I suspect the ocean cannot hold them all. But birth poems? Are there any? Perhaps the first and last words on the subject suffice: *I will greatly multiply your pain in childbearing, in pain you shall bring forth children.*

No illusions here. No dream sequences. Just brute and primitive nature; a return to our animal selves. Rather, a return to *their* animal selves, our curse being something else entirely: toil. But I don't think that's entirely correct. Maybe our curse is more bound up in their curse than we realize. Is it not ironic that the act that brings about conception, and the act that brings about birth, share the same form? The naked, spread legs; the desperate moans; the shut eyes and the grasping fingers? And yet, the two experiences could not be more different. Perhaps that's man's curse; forced to play the passive bystander, to be the 12th man on the bench, *but to have once been the star.* To be stripped, like the lover on the hospital bed, of illusions and phantoms, and to be thrust into the very core of reality itself.

And then the child is out, a screaming mass of red flesh and matted black hair. The nurses wrap him in a towel and, for unknown reasons, hand him to *me*. To me, he who has done nothing, or at least next to nothing. I look down at this fleshy, moist mass, this hysterical, screaming incarnate being, and feel— next to nothing. Oh, how I want my spirit to soar. How I want this moment to be a revelation of something, to represent something, for him to carry within his very being some meaning for me and my life. Is that too much to ask of an 8-pound, 6-ounce blob of flesh? I glance down at him and he closes his eyes and screams.

The nurse smiles, takes the boy from my arms, unwraps him, and places him on his mother's moist, full breasts. And she, hair wet with sweat, body still trembling, looks down at the boy and smiles, a smile not of this world. The boy stops screaming and looks up—I mean really looks—at his mother, and their eyes meet, and she begins to weep. Not tears of sadness or grief or loss, but tears that must have sat in an Edenic pool of pure joy for millions of years. And now her entire being glows with the goodness of life, and the awe-inspiring power of being. She lies there in utter harmony with the world, with existence itself, as if her entire existence was made for this moment right here. No, no, more than that; as if Earth and all her sister planets were made for this moment; no, even more than that, as if this galaxy and every galaxy and being itself was created, propped up, made to spin and spin and spin for just this one moment. Right here. In room 212 at Northwestern Medicine.

As for me, I merely sit there, a passive bystander to this cosmic dance. Once again, as always, a passive bystander.

* * *

When Michael completed his first three-peat, the city was enthralled. Michael was young, in the prime of his life and his game. We talked about six in a row; perhaps more. There seemed no limit to what he could accomplish.

And then tragedy struck. His father was murdered.

Murdered. Even now the word does not seem to fit. Drug dealers are murdered. Gang members are murdered. Low life bookies are murdered. But Michael's dad, the father of a god, senselessly and stupidly murdered? Reality seemed to come crashing down.

That Michael's dad was murdered seemed unbelievable; equally unbelievable was the impact it clearly had on him. If Michael were a mere mortal, one would expect him, obviously, to be immensely impacted by so hideous an event. But Michael was not a mere mortal. So, the impact of the murder on Michael—the subsequent retirement from basketball, and entry into *minor league baseball!*—appeared at first impossible. It seemed to indicate a crack in the wall of illusion. Perhaps Michael was mortal like any other man.

Perhaps he bled real blood and cried real tears. Watching him play baseball, his slightly awkward 6' 6" frame not quite natural on a baseball diamond, certainly provided some fuel to that assessment.

But on further consideration, I decided that Michael's relationship with his father, James, and his first retirement from the game and sense of loss and ennui, was only further proof of his greatness. That Michael could have such a relationship with his father, could enjoy his father's company, look to him for advice, confide in him his deepest doubts and insecurities, this itself seemed almost mythical. Poem worthy. Like Burns's "My Father Was a Farmer": *He bade me act a manly part, though I had ne'er a farthing, O; For without an honest manly heart, no man was worth regarding, O.* Or Cummings's "my father moved through dooms of love:"

> *My father moved through theys of we,*
> *singing each new leaf out of each tree*
> *(and every child was sure that spring*
> *danced when she heard my father sing)*

But as for me, I never knew my father, he having left and moved across country, to that god-forsaken city known by its initials, LA, when I was only eight months old, or so I'm told. And I dare say I can't think of a single childhood friend who knew their father, I mean *really knew their father.* The idea of a father, thus, has always been as abstract for me as God the Father himself. And Michael's relationship with James mythical; transcendent.

But then suddenly I found myself a father. Myself. A father.

* * *

If only heroism were a single act; if only a single brave choice, etched in stone for all eternity, could make you a man. I could be a hero then, I think. One moment, even if awful, even if it meant annihilation, I could do that.

Standing before Caesar: *pledge thine allegiance or face the lions!* I think I could face the lions. Sure, it'd be terrible (hopefully old Leo wouldn't tear off my limbs one by one; a single bite to the neck would suffice), but doable.

Or if my commander screamed out, *Charge the Huns!* I think I could ascend the ladder from the trench, artillery exploding all around me, if I knew a shell was going to blast me to pieces within minutes. I could charge like a rhino then.

But heroism isn't like that, notwithstanding the poets' romanticism. More likely a stray bullet hits you in the groin, and you go down. For the next 18 hours you lie there, mutilated bodies and shit and flies all around you, artillery shells deafening, the pain nauseating, the fear even worse. And when the battle ends, a Hun takes you captive, and you become a POW, where you receive terrible medical care, terrible food, and no camaraderie. When the war ends three years later and you're released, you have permanent PTSD, a gut condition that makes you shit your pants whenever you eat something other than stale bread, and you're impotent. Jake Barnes looks downright pleasant next to you. Perhaps Eliot can be forgiven *The Waste Land* under these conditions?

One moment, one heroic "yes," I could do that. I know I could. But death by 100,000 pin pricks?

Everybody romanticizes Michael's shot over Russell. *I romanticize Michael's shot over Russell.* But Michael never makes that shot without the 1 billion, 395 million, 625 thousand practice shots he took in an empty gym before that shot. I *know* that's character. But that doesn't mean I can live it.

We rented one side of a duplex together, Lenore and me. There was one bedroom on the main floor, and another bedroom in the basement. I took the bedroom in the basement. Seeing we didn't know each other, really, we thought this arrangement would be less awkward. Would give us the chance to get to know one another.

It actually went surprisingly well. I give Lenore all the credit on that front. Bit by bit, day by day, we discovered that we kind of liked one another, that we *got along,* as they say. We even had some points of commonality. Besides the obvious insurance connection, we discovered that we both loved pizza (me sausage and pepperoni, Lenore straight pepperoni), '80s action movies (I am partial to Sly Stallone, Lenore to Harrison Ford), and crossword puzzles. Perhaps this all seems trivial. But life is comprised of trivialities. It's the glue that holds the whole world together; just look at contemporary poetry: you're more likely to read a poem about the physical qualities of Welch's grape jelly than about the metaphysical underpinnings of reality. So be it. Who can have a PB&J without grape jelly?

In any event, it was all going pretty well, and then the baby came.

I shouldn't call him "baby." Jeffrey was born. Lenore, ever the astute observer (she, not me, should be the poet), wanted to give him a name that would have meaning to me. I think she sensed my hesitation and fear around children—we'd babysat her nieces a couple of times—and thought a meaningful name might in some way bond us together. She also knew my obsession with Michael (could it have been the life-size cutout of him in my bedroom?)

She had first suggested Michael, and then Jordan, but I couldn't do it. I have read that there are some poems that the poet refuses to write down, that exist only in some deified realm in the poet's own mind, because to write them down would be to diminish them; defile them in some sense. I couldn't bring myself to name my son Michael or Jordan. It was just too much. But then Lenore did some further digging and suggested "Jeffrey," Michael's middle name. What can I say; Lenore is brilliant. Only the most hardcore fans would know Michael's middle name, and who would make the connection? The pressure would be off. Yet, I would be giving homage to the Greatest of All Time. So, Jeffrey it was.

But a great name does not make a great kid. That's not fair. The kid was not the problem. *I* was the problem. But either way, there was a problem.

Is not rearing children supposed to be the most meaningfully wonderful thing you can do in life? It's your legacy, right? Millions and billions of family photos over the years show smiling, happy children and smiling, happy parents. That's how it *is*, right? Or at least how *it's supposed to be*. Didn't God himself, you know, the maker of the universe, realize that parenting is where it's at; so, he had himself a son, Jesus?

Or is this all an illusion? These photos etched like poems in stone, portraying a moment that is not real?

What was the problem? I just did not feel … connected. I had hoped there would be a natural connection, perhaps even a biological connection. Things with Lenore had gone surprisingly well and had given me optimism that parenthood would go likewise. For Lenore, it did. She took to motherhood like a sparrow to a nest. But me, my twin demons of fear of commitment and fear of banality overwhelmed me. You know, that old fear of 2 o'clock in the afternoon? Who am I; why am I; what the hell am I supposed to do now? A sort of nausea and cloud of existential unknowingness.

People talk about the terror of 3 A.M. Bullshit. I suspect that most of the greatest poems were written at 3 A.M. The sense of existential certainty; of meaning, purpose, and drive is perhaps at its height at 3 A.M. But 2 P.M.? Could you imagine Poe writing "The Raven" at 2 P.M.? Surely not. Or what about those 2 P.M. NBA weekend start times? Those games are enough to send you into an existential tailspin; I stopped watching NBA afternoon games because of the sudden onset of ennui they caused.

But you think that's disorienting, try watching a two-month-old at 2 in the afternoon as the mother goes out for the first time to *stretch her legs*, and *get a break*. No problem, right? You can handle two hours alone with your son? And besides, it's nap time. All you need to do is sit in the La-Z-Boy in the next room watching Sly Stallone shoot up the commies until mom gets back. Couldn't be easier, right?

Wrong. You put the DVD in, grab the bowl of extra butter microwave movie popcorn from the kitchen table, and sit in the blue La-Z-Boy. Grab the handle on the side of the chair to recline when, suddenly, *whaaaaaaaaaa*. You arise, walk over to the baby's room, peak inside, see the baby tossing and turning and wailing. Walk into the room, pop the nook into the baby's mouth, and watch the baby suck the nook, suck the nook, and seemingly fall back asleep. Turn to leave, when, suddenly, *creeaaaaaak*, the 1940s-era oak flooring bellows. The baby's eyes lurch open, the nook drops out, the baby screams. You pick the baby up, pat pat pat on the bottom, nook in mouth, sway back and forth back and forth. The baby's eyes flutter, heavy, open and close, open and close. Close. You lean over the side of the wood-slatted crib, begin to set the baby down, but just before flesh hits mattress, baby's eyes lurch open, nook drops out, baby screams and screams.

You grab the nook, go to the kitchen, glance at the digital clock on the wall, 2:04, find the "emergency" bottle of pumped breastmilk bring the bottle to the mouth, watch the baby resist, tossing head side to side, side to side. Set the bottle down. Pop the nook in mouth. Inadvertently look over at the digital clock on the wall. 2:04. Grab a blanket from baby's room, drape it over your shoulder and baby's head, stride from kitchen to living room, living room to kitchen, exactly 13 paces. Kitchen to living room, living room to kitchen. Stop in kitchen. Quietly, ever so quietly, lift the blanket off of shoulder, glance at baby. Baby's eyes are closed. Baby's breathing is heavy. Baby is asleep.

Tiptoe back to baby's crib. Transfer baby from forearms to hands. Gently, ever so gently, ever so softly, like a helicopter landing, place the baby in the crib. Nook in mouth. Stand there. Wait there. All quiet on the western front. Turn to leave (avoid the creaky floorboard), exit through the doorway, look up at the digital clock, 2:06, look back at baby, quiet baby, sleeping baby. Turn to walk back to Stallone when, *waaaaaaaaaaah!!!* Look up at clock. 2:06.

Grab the baby, grab the nook, grab the blanket, exit through the front door onto the porch. Grab the stroller. Exit porch door. Outside, the day is brilliant. The sun shining. The oak leaves orange and brilliant. The air fresh. Descend the steps to the sidewalk. Place the baby (still screaming) into the stroller. Strap the baby (still screaming) safely into the stroller. Glance at watch. 2:08. Begin to walk. But to where? And for what? Purposeful runners are out in droves, Nike shoes, North Face tees, legs laced with sinuous muscles. Old men too, mustached, wearing Homburgs and tennis shoes, a coffee in their right hand, newspaper under left armpit, strolling to the park, alone, alone, alone. Mothers pass by. Too many to count. Slender. Pony-tailed. Lithe. Skin glowing. Perfect breasts squashed in tight sport bras, undulating in the rhythmic rise and fall of lithe legs. All pushing strollers, some doubles, faces purposefully set, but not aggressively so. Their happy kids tucked inside, asleep, or quietly watching the world pass by. These mothers an image of competence and grace.

And then there's me. Sweatpants still on. *Sweatpants?* Wrinkled 97-98 championship tee with cartoon faces of Michael, Scottie, and Dennis. Three-day stubble. Baby screaming, piercing the perfect day with august angst. A haggard (terrified?) expression on my face. Glance at watch. 2:10.

You get the picture.

When Lenore returns at 4, she is glowing. Nails done afresh. Hair washed and trimmed, smelling of an ocean breeze. Her perfect teeth visible behind a joyful smile. Until she sees you and the baby.

The baby's face red and mottled from screaming. Your face, red and mottled from terror. Your nerves fried. Trying, yet again, to force down some milk to get the baby to stop screaming just stop screaming.

Mother strides to the baby, strides to the rescue, takes the baby in hand, holds baby up to her face and says, ever so calmly, *it's ok, you're safe now, mommy's here,* unfurls a left breast in an unhurried yet efficient manner, plugs the baby's face onto the nip, and walks out of the room. Baby is asleep, and sleeping peacefully in his crib, within minutes.

I know it was wrong, but I took to avoiding the baby.

* * *

I began hiding out in my part of the duplex, only ascending when I knew (or was pretty certain) he was sleeping. I'd casually say where's *Jeffrey,* pretending to look around for him. She'd respond, *sssshhhh,* he's sleeping. I'd respond *oh, ok, well what do you want to do?* But I soon realized this ruse was not particularly effective, at least so much as it afforded me an opportunity to be with Lenore sans child, because Lenore only ever wanted to nap, or go to bed when Jeffrey was sleeping. I don't blame her; from what I heard at night, he was a terrible sleeper.

I thus stood at the threshold of Frost's divergent roads. I knew, perhaps instinctively, that my one path to happiness, the way out of myself and self-induced misery and interiority was Lenore; also, that the way to Lenore was through Jeffrey. Yet another path emerged, one well-trod; seemingly easily traversed. But I had walked that path for ages past and knew that upon setting foot on it I would sink up to my navel. This was the path of Self; of the endless loop of the inner monologue that is no loop, no movement at all, but a stinking quagmire. Yet, if you think that the choice was easy, all light, goodness, peace, joy, hope, and happiness on the one side, and misery, gloom, doom, and darkness on the other, and surely surely surely I must choose the former, then you know nothing of human nature.

Is Michael the anomaly, or is most everyone else in the human race the anomaly? If basketball had never been invented, would Michael still have become great? Is he great because of the game, or is he just great? Very few people are great. Very few people are even good.

I chose the road more traveled by.

But Lenore—patient, lovely, magnificent Lenore—had her limits. About nine months in, Jeffrey colicky, screaming for hours on end, arching his back in misery, Lenore turned to me and said *aren't you ever going to do anything?* Her words hit me like one of those infamous Michael tongue-lashings he'd give out during practice; awakened out of my several-months haze, I boldly responded, *yes, I will take him to the Bulls game tonight!*

* * *

As soon as we'd begun backing out of the driveway, I knew I'd made a mistake. It took close to an hour to get Jeffrey's diaper bag packed. It was now 6:15. Tipoff was 7. And we had over an hour drive to get to United Center.

And while Jeffrey had calmed down, and miraculously gone into the car seat without a fuss, once I put the car into reverse and began slowly backing up, he began to wail a primal scream as if he were in the mouth of a saber-toothed tiger being carried away from his mother.

Perhaps Jeffrey sensed my own nervousness and incompetence; they say dogs have a sixth (or even seventh) sense. Perhaps his fear was justified; no, surely his fear was justified.

I placed the car in drive, exhaled, and began moving forward.

If I had been driving toward something good, or even moderately watchable, I might have been able to maintain my initial enthusiasm aimed at Lenore. But the intervening years since 97-98 had not been kind to the Bulls. In fact, we were in the midst of our worst season ever.

Elton Brand was passable as a basketball player, but one of our new Big Three was a guy who changed his name to Metta World Peace. Really? Sure, we had come to enjoy the antics of Dennis. But only because he was good; really good. But Metta World Peace?

We'd gone from winning 72, then 69, then 62 from 95-96, 96-97, then 97-98, respectively, to 13 games (strike-shortened), 17, and finally 15 games in 2000-2001.

If only I were a real poet, how I would make an epic poem devouring Jerry Krause! Milton's Satan would seem a puppy compared to Krause, that Napoleonic porker whose pants perpetually tucked his belly button into bed and who looked like a door-to-door butter salesman rather than a basketball executive. Oh, how I wish Grendel would have risen from the swamp to devour the monomaniacal idiot. Fifteen games! Metta World Peace! This is your strategy? You blew up the Greatest Team of All Time for this; for a chance to put Bryce Drew, Khalid El-Amin, Jake Voskuhl, and Fred Hoiberg on the court?

I know it is dangerous and self-defeating for a Straight, White Male to wax eloquent about the past. But bear with me for just a moment. There was something cruel about the turn of events. It was the year 2000. The millennial year. We had all just escaped Y2K unscathed. Hope was in the air; the good life for all was within grasp. Personal computers would soon land in everyone's living rooms! Hurray!

But for me? I looked in the rearview mirror. I could not see Jeffrey, but I could hear him. I couldn't help but think of this moment as a metaphor for my life. I exhaled deeply as I drove toward United Center.

I likewise could not help but think of the Bulls as a metaphor for my life. It didn't help that the hated Lakers had just won the first of what would be their own three-peat, thoroughly making the Bulls and Michael a distant memory. It was all Kobe and Shaq now, notwithstanding that Kobe owed Michael everything. Everything.

While the Millennium seemed like the beginning for most everyone around me, for me, it was beginning to look more and more like the end.

As soon as I sat in my seat at United Center, I felt a deep dread. I again knew this was a terrible mistake. I was only half a quarter late, but already the Bulls were down 18 points. And that beacon of World Peace had, again, been tossed from the game for a fragrant foul. Ironies of irony.

If that weren't enough, Jeffrey again began howling. And not the fussy, squirmy stuff of almost one-year-olds. No, no, the all-out bellowing, screaming, *would somebody please rescue me from this madman, he has kidnapped me from my mother* sort of screaming. I thought being trapped in my own home with a screaming baby was life's low point; turns out not by a long shot. The only thing I can think of that would be worse is sitting on a flight while Jeffrey wails and wails, and there, just a couple of rows ahead, in First Class, sits Michael.

The game being what it was, and Jeffrey being who he was, I was tempted to abandon all hope right there and succumb to misery and introspection.

But then suddenly, a wave of nostalgia swept over me. Perhaps it was the smell of stale beer all around me. Or maybe the familiar and joyous sound of Ray Clay's voice over the PA system.

I didn't often go to Bulls games, ticket prices being what they were during the Glory Days. But when I did go, I usually went alone, sitting high up in the third deck. These were the best moments of my life. I'd buy a 16-ounce Miller and a bag of peanuts (unshelled) and simply revel in it all. It was one of those few places where one could really lose oneself, in a good way. A fully immersive experience in another world, another mode of being. Where, fact or fiction, this thing—this game—just a few feet away, was important. No, was all important. That who won mattered. Sure, this was no Napoleonic war: the loser wasn't scraped off the court at the end and buried six feet under. But something more than mere existing took place on that court. Some vital remainder of man's enchanted past lived on. Where even an uber self-conscious postmodern such as I could lose himself outside himself if only for a couple hours. Sure, these moments didn't last; we all had to go home at the end of the night and face our nightmares once again. But they were glorious whilst they lasted.

I arose from my seat, Jeffrey in my left arm (still screaming) and walked to the concession stand. The cashier, who looked so much like a young Jerry Krause that I did a double take, looked at me, smiled wryly, and said *Enjoying the game, huh?* I ignored the comment and ordered a Miller and a bag of peanuts. I paid for my items (somehow $10 more than when the Bulls were good; how was this possible? This is not how capitalism is supposed to work), and sat back down. I attempted to get into that ideal state of being where, even amidst the screaming child and the terrible Bulls, I could enjoy the moment. But then I took a swig of the beer. *Fucking PBR!* I wanted to scream. That pimply, wannabe Jerry Krause screwed up my order! Oh how quickly our illusions turn to delusions. Our nostalgia turns acidic.

You can never return to your childhood home.

The past is passed.

All return is hopeless.

The peanuts were better than the beer.

But the Bulls were still terrible.

And Jeffrey continued to wail.

He now appeared to be hungry, reaching for every shelled peanut I tossed in my mouth. I looked at my feet. Misery of miseries! I'd left the diaper bag in the car.

I shelled a peanut, split it down the middle, and bit off half of what was left. I placed the small remainder in Jeffrey's mouth. Instantly he stopped screaming.

Are our lives to be measured by discrete moments, or the generic whole? Are some seconds worth more than others?

Michael takes the ball, dribble dribble dribble, drives right (does *not* push Russell. Watch it again. He was *falling over*), leaps, flicks the wrist, the ball hovers, it hangs there, I swear, time stops, watch it, I tell you, watch it, for just a nanosecond, time stops, the ball hovers, then drops, through the net. Pandemonium!!!

And me? And me? And me?

He fumble s with the peanut, the defense grabs for it, he flicks the fingers away (gently, ever so gently), there, finally, it's shelled, the defense reaches again, he concedes, hands it over, there, the peanut is in the mouth—and and and—suddenly, the face turns blotchy, red circles like mosquito bites form, and the defense is gasping for air, gasping for breath, gasping for life.

Oh no, I think, it must be lodged in his throat, cutting off airway. So, I turn him over, bam bam bam on his back. Nothing. From red in the face to now a light blue. What is happening? Am I killing this child? It is clear he is not getting oxygen.

Frantically, I begin waving my arms, yelling for help. The smattering of Bulls fans around me, wearing Michael and Dennis and Steve Kerr jerseys (but not Scottie jerseys; note, not Scottie jerseys), stare at me dumbly, wondering, what's gotten into this nut? Nut! That's it! Hadn't Lenore told me never to feed Jeffrey a nut until he was 2, or was it 6, or 16? Things are not looking good. Jeffrey is, it seems, unable to breathe.

Is this how it ends? Not with a bang but a whimper?

No, not even a whimper; silence.

What is one second? Long enough to make you a legend?

What is one second? Long enough to make a life?

What is one second? Long enough to make you a murderer?

Suddenly, I feel Jeffrey being yanked from my arms. I look. A muscular man with a buzzcut who looks like he could be a trainer for the Bulls yells *he's going into anaphylaxis shock. Get the paramedics!*

It's all a whirl after that. The man starts doing baby CPR. Composed, orderly, a consummate pro. I tried to end a life; he clearly knows how to save one. I stand there, dazed. But soon get the sense that I am being watched. I look up at the jumbotron, and there I am. I stand there, looking at myself looking at myself. Seeing myself from outside myself. But alas, I am still thoroughly within myself.

Then I look down, toward the court, and see that the game has stopped. All the players are looking up at the jumbotron. A few are on their knees, clearly praying.

Suddenly I'm surrounded by athletic men and ripped women wearing ponytails. One of the men reaches into a bag and pulls out a mini-rocket toy looking thing, grabs the fleshy parts of Jeffrey's left thigh, and jabs the rockety thing onto the flesh. And finally, as if by some magic or miracle, Jeffrey lets out a bellowing scream, louder than I've ever heard.

Someone yells at me *are you dad*, and I nod my head stupidly and then feel myself being led up the stairs toward the concourse, but just before I exit, I hear the clapping of thousands of fans, clapping surely not for me, but for the medical folks competent enough to do something with their lives.

Then I was ushered into an ambulance, its red lights spinning and blaring, and I saw Jeffrey lying on a medical cot, an oxygen mask over his face, no longer blue, but still with those awful splotches covering his face.

And then the back doors closed, and we drove off.

* * *

I don't blame Lenore for ending it after that fiasco. She'd given me more than my fair shake, but this was the final straw. A quixotic degree of incompetence and stupidity. She was willing to sacrifice her own life, to give up her desires and hopes for me; but she wasn't willing to sacrifice Jeffrey. That was too much. And I could no longer be trusted (could I ever be trusted?).

I learned after the fact that she'd watched the whole thing unfold on TNT. Even though not a Bulls fan in the least, she'd turned the game on to see what her boys were up to. Only to have to sit there in horror as she saw her son's life unraveling before her eyes.

What helplessness; what panic; what fear. She might have even beat us to the hospital.

Jeffrey turned out fine. An allergy to peanuts. But he was a minute or less from dying. One minute.

There wasn't a great fight scene or even a shouting match. She just calmly and quietly told me that I had to go. That it wasn't going to work. That she was sorry (she was sorry!) for everything, but she couldn't do it anymore.

I told her I understood. That I was a pathetic loser who was the one who needed to apologize. That I just wasn't cut out for this life.

In the end, I went gently into the night.

* * *

Over the next nine years, I tried a great many things to, as they say, find *meaning* and *purpose*. I took a poetry workshop at the local library, but found that I was the only one who wrote in meter and verse. The other workshop participants, mostly 20-something MFA grads who worked at Starbucks, looked at me like I was a slave owner or something when they heard my poems. For their part, their poems all had lines like *love is love the feeling of which makes my skin burn like the tropics. The science of love is real you see; a burning at the equator of the human form which has no form.*

I couldn't take it, so I quit.

I tried traveling. I thought perhaps that traveling to some exotic locale could snap me out of my doldrums. That if the material self changed zones, the immaterial self might follow suit. So, I picked the most exotic locale I could think of: Indonesia. But when I got there and began walking around, I realized I had made a terrible mistake. I thought Chicago was a big, overcrowded city. But it was nothing compared to Jakarta. Wordsworth's daffodils may have given him supreme company; for my part, I wandered lonely as a cloud, even in the massive crowds of milling Indonesians. Alas, my self had booked a flight with me.

I spent a couple of days in my hotel room watching English-dubbed television and eating fast food. Then I booked an early flight back home.

I even tried going to church. Why? I'm not really sure. I didn't grow up in a religious house. But I'd seen old movies and saw something poetic in those old Christian churches. And not just the bells and smoke and candles; but in the people themselves. The bowing and kneeling and rising. And silence. Maybe that most. The silence.

So, I went to the local Catholic church, but found nothing of what I'd hoped for. Perhaps it was all the dads dressed in Polo shirts and Dockers. No suits and ties here. Or maybe the vernacular over the Latin; I'd forgotten that. Or maybe it was simply the place itself, which looked more like a Soviet-era government building than a place of worship. But more likely it was the beholder rather than the beheld that was the problem. Whatever the case, I felt none of what Larkin described: *It pleases me to stand in silence here.* Then again, maybe that's it; maybe it was the simple lack of silence; if I'd gone when I was sure there was nothing going on, when only the air and I were there, would that have made a difference? Probably not.

I sent notes to Lenore from time to time, and gifts to Jeffrey. But I never tried to visit. It seemed better that way; better for everyone if I was never seen again.

My life took on a predictable, routinized existence. Work, a bit of poetry (always the old stuff, the older the better) over takeout, and then old Bulls' games until I fell asleep (I had the complete seasons from every year Michael played for the Bulls).

I might have remained in this state, might still be in it today, if not for Michael. Perhaps it is fitting; he that was the cause of so many of my illusions, was also the Thor-like hammer that broke them, or at least cracked them.

It was an hour-long interview Michael gave to Michael Wilbon in 2009. I waited for it with great anticipation. I suppose I was hoping to relive some of the Glory Days. To see something of the past revivified. To be reminded of greatness, or at least the possibility of greatness.

But again, the milk had soured.

Perhaps it was Michael's general flabbiness. He certainly was not fat by any measure, but he was flabby. Softening like butter left on the counter.

Or maybe it was his eyes, somehow disconcertingly yellowed; one wondered if they'd glow in the dark.

But most likely it was the words uttered from Michael's own mouth. His own refusal to be anything other than human. Full acknowledgment of his flaws: a divorce, gambling, rancor with teammates. He said he never asked to be a superhero. He was just a guy. Who loved basketball, who was driven to extremes to play basketball. Who had a singular focus and energy that he harnessed to become a great basketball player, but that was it. He never asked to be, and did not pretend to be, a god, or even a role model. He was just a guy.

Just a guy. Just a guy.

We are all of us, all of us, the lot of us, just guys and gals; mere flesh upon mere bones; floating on a bright blue globe in an enormous cosmos. Capable of so little and yet.

So, I called her. I mean I actually *called* her, didn't text.

I was expecting (hoping?) it would go to voicemail. I would leave a message and run panting to my room, pull the covers over my head, and hide. But to my surprise, she answered on the second ring. Also to my surprise, her voice didn't sound surprised or even angry. Her voice, that voice I hadn't heard in years, the slight huskiness, even gravelly tones betraying an immense toughness I knew she possessed. We exchanged pleasantries, and then I spit it out. *I'd like to see him.*

I explained that I knew I didn't have the right. That I was pathetic and horrible and should have done more, been more, these past 9 years. But if I could just see him, even for a moment, from a distance, just to lay eyes upon him, maybe it would help me sort myself.

She interrupted me then to say that would be nice. He'd like that. She explained that he had a basketball game the following week, in my neighborhood. She wouldn't be going. But he'd love it if I could go. He asks about you. He has a picture; you and him. Remember? *Where you're wearing matching Jordan jerseys?*

I didn't know how to respond, so I simply said Great. I'll be there.

* * *

Which is how I find myself, now, sitting on this wooden bleacher at John Glenn Grade School, the distinct smell of 10-year-boy body odor and stale popcorn hanging in the air, feeling those butterflies that feel more like dragonflies in my gut, more nervous than, than, than I've ever been in my life.

Self-doubting, self-loathing, and yet: hopeful.

And now the locker room door bursts open and a mass and jumble of red jerseys pile out dribbling and stumbling, as I wonder will I recognize him? Will he recognize me? And now I see, like looking at me, with the best parts of her. Could we yet be we?

I sit and stare, looking over there, at him, in the gym, the movement, the grace, no Michael, but that face—that face—that face. It is turning now, eyes blue, brow furrowed, he scans, and then, a glance. It is only a glance, one look, but not by chance. Our eyes meet, he puts the ball under his left arm and waves. At me. Then turns and dribbles off.

It is only one glance; a mere glance; one look. Signifying?

Sugarloaf December
For Mike Twistle Entwistle

Alpenglow spilled on dimming day,
ineluctable wind across evening,
solstice moon turning toward winter.

Pack buckles singing, skis shouldered,
we trudge up the last hundred meters,
you humming Marley and Toots.

Hard-packed, ear-rasping snow,
creaking brittle under our boots,
wind-slung like darts into watery eyes.

Cold flows easily, artery and vein,
heart and spleen, kidney and lungs,
hallowed air and drifted ground.

In the lift shack at the top of Spillway,
our home for the short, bitter night,
the anemometer never dips below sixty.

Skies clear, temperature plummets,
portending flesh-devouring gales
in the weak, rose light of the dawn.

In the howl of midnight, a groomer
bursts in to record the wind speed,
astonished that we can sleep.

With first light splashing the summit,
twenty-two below bone zero,
we smile at our rare good fortune.

Our tracks will leave no trace in
the wind-burnished snow, polished
as white and bone-hard as an antler.

Clicked in, we slide down Narrow Gauge,
along the length of wind-savaged fences,
and radio that there will be no race today.

Bruce Pratt

Skating With The Eagle

I spied the bone-white head,
sweeping dark wings, in summer,
a soaring shadow on the fields,
lost as he rose above the woods.

When he appears overhead,
the rooster drives the hens
into the barn with a riot
of crowing and beating wings,

chickadees abandon
swinging feeders to
hide in the mock orange,
or flee to alder thickets.

Today as I skated the pond,
his great span gyred above,
broad, silent, backlit shadow
shadowing mine along the ice.

Bruce Pratt

Cloud Skating

For John B. Lee

Cirrus clouds,
fat, grey bullfrogs,
empyrean swimmers,
in full extension,
breaststroke eastward
on a west wind.

Gusts and they morph,
become hockey players,
circling the rink pregame,
tapping their goalie's pads,
dreaming of open nets.

Sun ends the game.

In the dressing room,
poets all, they kill the first
case of local brew,
Al Purdy, Richard Harrison,
Randy Maggs, and John B. Lee,
who's played his third
game of the day.

Even the refs and linesmen
get cold ones because, hell
everybody blows a call,
or rips a wrister wide,
when the goalie's face down
like a squashed spider,
or pulled for the extra attacker
in the dying minutes of
the third period and ends up
staring into this clear blue.

Bruce Pratt

Contributors' Notes

David Atkinson, currently Professor and President Emeritus at MacEwan University in Edmonton, Canada, has served as President of four Canadian universities and Dean at two others. Although having published over 100 papers and five books, he is a newcomer to Sport and Literature, and draws on his college experiences as a distance runner in writing about Parker's *Once a Runner*. He was an All American at Indiana University, competed internationally for Canada, and was recognized as Canada's Outstanding University Track and Field Athlete.

Sam Barbee's work has appeared in many periodicals, including *Poetry South, Crucible, Asheville Poetry Review, Southern Poetry Anthology VII, Georgia Journal, Kakalak, Pembroke Magazine, Vox Poetica, and Courtland Review*. His second poetry collection, That Rain We Needed (2016, Press 53), was a nominee for the Roanoke-Chowan Award as one of North Carolina's best poetry collections of 2016. He was awarded an "Emerging Artist's Grant" from the Winston-Salem Arts Council to publish his first collection *Changes of Venue* (Mount Olive Press) and has been a featured poet on the North Carolina Public Radio Station WFDD. He received the 59th Poet Laureate Award from the North Carolina Poetry Society for his poem "The Blood Watch."

Adam Berlin is the author of four novels, including *Belmondo Style* (St. Martin's Press/ winner of The Publishing Triangle's Ferro-Grumley Award) and *Both Members of the Club* (Texas A&M University Consortium Press/winner of the Clay Reynolds Novella Prize), and a collection of boxing poems *The Standing Eight*. He teaches writing at John Jay College of Criminal Justice in New York City and co-edits the litmag *J Journal: New Writing on Justice*.

RF Brown is a house husband and a recreational Cultural Theorist. He/Him is an alumnx of Hampshire College. His stories with the theme of sports as semiotic language systems have been published in *Aethlon's* Special Issue: Teaching Sport Literature, *Spitball, White Wall, Sucker,* and *Foglifter*. RFBrown.net and @rfbrownwards.

Rick Campbell is a poet and essayist living on Alligator Point, Florida. His most recent collection of poems is *Provenance* (Blue Horse Press). He's published six other poetry books as well as poems and essays in journals including *The Georgia Review, Fourth River, Kestrel,* and *New Madrid*. He's won a Pushcart Prize and a NEA Fellowship in Poetry. He teaches in the Sierra Nevada College MFA Program.

Bob Carlton (Twitter @bobcarlton3) lives and works in Leander, TX.

Tadhg Coakley is the Cork-based award-winning author of *The First Sunday in September* (a sports novel) and *Whatever It Takes* (a crime novel). *Everything* (a sports autobiography, which he co-wrote with its subject, Denis Coughlan) was one of the 2020 sports books of the year in *The Sunday Times, The Irish Examiner* and *The Irish Times*. His short stories, articles and essays have been widely published. He writes on sport for *The Irish Examiner*. www.tadhgcoakley.ie.

Jacob Cohen is the author of short stories and this tale you are about to read, Morton's Toe. He began writing as a child but steered away after meeting his wife of 14 years and having two children. Basketball was an early passion of his. He began playing as a child and still tinkers around today. He previously published "Spaghetti Incident" in September of 2021.

Salvatore Difalco is the author of 5 books. Recent work has appeared in *Brilliant Flash Fiction, Cafe Irreal* and *Gone Lawn*.

David Evans, Jr. lives in Southern Illinois and teaches at John A. Logan College. He has published a chapbook, *Shadow Boxer*, from Finishing Line Press. He hopes to publish a book of poems, *Flicking Jabs at the Universe*, soon.

Dr. Anne Greenawalt is a writer, competitive swimmer, trail adventurer, and educator. She earned a doctorate in Adult Education from Penn State University and a master's degree in Creative Writing: Prose from the University of East Anglia, and works as the training manager for a nonprofit that provides residential and clinical services for youths who have experienced trauma. Engage with her on Twitter at @dr_greenawalt and visit her website at http://www.annegreenawalt.com.

Albert Haley's poems have appeared in *Poems & Plays, New Texas, The Anglican Theological Review*, and elsewhere. He is a past winner of the Rattle Poetry Prize. Since 1997 he has served as writer in residence at Abilene Christian University in Abilene, Texas.

Robert Hamblin is now retired after fifty years of teaching at Southeast Missouri State University. He is the author or editor of forty-two books, including ten volumes of poems, the latest being *Plutarch Redux: Parallel Poems in the Age of Trump*. He served as poetry editor for *Aethlon* from 1984 until 2005.

Robert Harlow played semi-pro hockey, in the pre-helmet years, where fisticuffs was the main action on the ice. He is the author of a book of poems, *Places Near And Far*, published by Louisiana Literature in 2018. He holds an MFA from University of Arizona and is retired from a life in carpentry and academia. Mr. Harlow now resides in upstate New York with his wife, ceramic artist Nancy Henry.

Dariusz Janczewski was born in Poland and emigrated to the United States in 1984. In 2021 Dariusz received his MA in English and Creative Writing program (MA) from Southern New Hampshire University. Most of his stories contain life experiences that are liberally fictionalized. Dariusz believes that writing has the capacity to instantly connect diverse and distant worlds in a way not possible by other media. Dariusz is also a freelance graphic designer working in Missoula, Montana. He shares his life with his wife Katie.

Anna Journey is the author of the poetry collections *The Judas Ear* (LSU Press, 2022), *The Atheist Wore Goat Silk* (LSU Press, 2017), *Vulgar Remedies* (LSU Press, 2013), and *If Birds Gather Your Hair for Nesting* (University of Georgia Press, 2009), which was selected by Thomas Lux for the National Poetry Series. She is an associate professor of English at the University of Southern California.

Professor of English and Creative Writing at Lock Haven University, **Marjorie Maddox** has published 11 collections of poetry—including *Transplant, Transport, Transubstantiation* (Yellowglen Prize); *Local News from Someplace Else; Perpendicular As I* (Sandstone Book Award)—the short story collection *What She Was Saying* (Fomite); four children's and YA books—including *Inside Out: Poems on Writing and Readiing Poems with Insider Exercises* (Finalist Children's Educational Category 2020 International Book Awards), and *A Crossing of Zebras: Animal Packs in Poetry; Rules of the Game: Baseball Poems, I'm Feeling Blue, Too!*—Common Wealth: *Contemporary Poets on Pennsylvania* (co-editor); *Presence: A Journal of Catholic Poetry* (assistant editor). She is the great grandniece of Branch Rickey, the general manager of the Brooklyn Dodgers who helped break the color barrier by signing Jackie Robinson to Major League Baseball. Published in 2021: her book *Begin with a Question* (Paraclete Press) and her ekphrastic collaboration with photographer Karen Elias, *Heart Speaks, Is Spoken For* (Shanti Arts). For more information, please see www.marjoriemaddox.com.

Jeffrey Munroe is the editor of the *Reformed Journal,* author of the book *Reading Buechner,* and a lifelong Detroit Tigers fan. He produced "Poet, Poet, You Stand Alone" in a poetry group led by Jack Ridl. He recently retired as the Executive Vice President of Western Theological Seminary.

Dave Nielsen is the author of *Unfinished Figures* (Lynx House Press, 2016). He lives in Salt Lake City. His dad played power forward for the University of Utah men's basketball team.

Scott Palmieri is a professor of English at Johnson & Wales University in Providence, Rhode Island. His writing has been published in *Sport Literate, Aethlon, Hobart, The Leaflet, The Alembic, and The Result Is What You See Today: Poems About Running.* He played baseball at Providence College and continues his love of the sport through writing, coaching Little League, and playing, as long as his legs will allow, in a senior men's league. He lives in Wakefield, Rhode Island, with his wife and three children, his biggest fans.

E. Martin Pedersen, originally from San Francisco, has lived for 40 years in eastern Sicily where he taught English at the local university. His poetry has appeared most recently in *Soundings East, Vox Poetica, LitBreak, Muddy River Poetry Review and Slab.* Martin is an alumnus of the Squaw Valley Community of Writers. His collection of haiku, *Bitter Pills,* has just come out. His poetry chapbook, *Exile's Choice,* is scheduled for publication by Kelsay Books, as is his collection, *Method and Madness,* by Odyssey Press. Martin blogs at: https://emartinpedersenwriter.blogspot.com.

Bruce Pratt is author of the novel *The Serpents of Blissfull* (Mountain State Press), *The Trash Detail: Stories* (New Rivers Press), the poetry collection *Boreal* (Antrim House), and the poetry chapbook *Forms and Shades* (Clare Songbirds Publishing). His work has appeared in the US, Canada, Ireland, and Wales and he edits *American Fiction*.

Thomas Reynolds is a Professor of English at Johnson County Community College in Overland Park, Kansas, and has published poems in various print and online journals, including *New Delta Review, Alabama Literary Review, Aethlon: The Journal of Sport Literature, Sport Literate, Spitball: The Literary Baseball Magazine, Flint Hills Review,* and *Prairie Poetry.* He is the author of three chapbooks: *Electricity* (1987), *The Kansas Hermit Poems* (2013) and *Small Town Rodeos* (2016). Woodley Memorial Press published his poetry collections *Ghost Town Almanac* (2008) and *Home Field* (2019).

Morgan Riedl is a doctoral student at Ohio University in Athens, Ohio, where she lives with her rez dog and retired horse (not in the house). She has an MA in creative nonfiction from Colorado State University. Her work has been featured in the *Normal School, Sonora Review,* and *Entropy.*

Jeffrey Wald writes, with frequent interruptions from his five boys, from the Twin Cities. His writing has appeared in periodicals such as *Dappled Things, Genealogies of Modernity,* and *The Short Humour Site.*

Made in the USA
Middletown, DE
27 February 2022